YOU
CAN'T
MAKE
ME
IF I
DON'T
WANT
TO

Books by

MOLLY CONE

Annie Annie
Crazy Mary
Hurry Henrietta
Mishmash
Mishmash and the Sauerkraut Mystery
Mishmash and the Substitute Teacher
Mishmash and Uncle Looey
The Other Side of the Fence
A Promise Is a Promise
The Real Dream
Reeney
Simon
The Trouble with Toby
You Can't Make Me If I Don't Want To

YOU CAN'T MAKE ME IF I DON'T WANT TO

MOLLY CONE

Illustrated by Marvin Friedman

Houghton Mifflin Company Boston 1971

To Ellen

chapter 1

I'M NOT GOING," Mitch said.

"You can be darn sure you're going," his father said emphatically. Everything Mitch's father did was emphatic. He walked as if he were in a hurry to get somewhere. He snapped his fingers when he talked. He talked loudly. His father had never had any doubts about anything at all, thought Mitch. 1690184

Mitch saw his cousin Bernie was listening. Bernie had been staying with them all summer. He was going to go right on staying with them — even after they went to Israel.

Bernie was sixteen, only two years older than Mitch. Mitch noticed that his father treated Bernie as an equal.

Mitch heard his mother's voice coming from the bedroom. His mother had been talking on the telephone most of the day — saying the same kinds of things over and over again. It seemed to Mitch that his mother had been on the telephone most of the time during the past week. When she was not saying good-bye to her friends, she was canceling things, or checking on things, or ordering things, or arranging things. For a whole month now, she had been continually busy cleaning the house, or showing the house, or worrying out loud what to pack and what to leave.

It didn't bother his mother to have Bernie as part of their family, reflected Mitch. It didn't change anything for her.

She had given Mitch's old comic books to Goodwill Industries, along with his tennis shoes and the jeans which he had cut off himself. All of his brother's stuff was being packed up and taken along: he was younger. Bernie could take anything he wanted: he was older. Mitch's opinions didn't seem to count. He was either "too young to know what he was talking about" or "old enough to know better."

"I'm not going," he said again, but no one paid any attention.

His father was standing on a kitchen chair, handing down the dishes from the top shelf. Mitch watched him and Bernie working together.

His father looked like just another kid — except that his hair was thinner than a kid's hair. Actually, it was easy to see that he was old, even though he wore tennis shoes and sloppy shirts and chewed gum.

His father's ambition was to "live like a human being" — whatever that meant. His mother's ambition was to stand up and be counted. All his life, Mitch had listened to his parents talk about going to Israel. Now they were really going. They were going for one year. To Mitch one year was as long as forever.

Everybody should have a goal, his parents thought. Going to Israel had always been their goal. If you didn't have a goal, you were just no good, that's what they thought. Mitch didn't have any goal. He just wanted to stay where he was.

Joe began to yammer. Joe was three years old; he talked baby talk.

"He wants something," Bernie said.

"What do you want?" his father said, listening carefully. "Say it again."

Say it again. Say it again. Nobody but Mitch could ever understand what Joe said. "He wants a drink of water," said Mitch, and filled a paper cup and gave it to him.

Joe drank some of it, loudly, and spilled the rest of it down his front.

"Oh for heaven's sake." His mother hurried in from the bedroom. She dabbed at Joe with a kitchen towel.

"It wasn't my fault," said Mitch.

"You haven't finished packing your things," she reminded. "One bag each. That's all we can take with us on the plane. Everything else we want has to be packed and shipped."

"You can be sure Bernie's stuff is ready to go," his father hinted loudly.

Bernie was neat; Bernie was never late; Bernie made his bed every morning. He didn't fall over his own feet or burn the tomato-soup pan or get shoe polish on the living room rug. He kept his fingernails clean and remembered to turn off the light in the bathroom.

"He doesn't dawdle around all day," his father said.

"I got plenty of time," mumbled Mitch, and he went into the dining room.

Two barrels full of stuff stood there. On the dining room table were some more things to be packed. The table top was permanently scarred with pieces of newspaper still stuck to the surface from Mitch's airplane glue. He had covered the whole table carefully with newspapers. But the tube of glue had leaked. It had leaked all night and soaked through. Every time his father looked at it, he yelled at him.

Mitch went back into the kitchen. "Who's going to be living here?"

"A nice couple," his mother said. "We're going to sign the lease tomorrow."

"What time you figure on leaving?" Mitch said after dinner. He didn't say "we." It would be a lie to say "we." His mother didn't notice. She was

4

busy dumping the chicken bones and the paper plates into the garbage sack.

"Six o'clock Tuesday," said his father.

"In the morning?"

"Of course, in the morning."

"That's exactly three o'clock in the afternoon in Israel," said Bernie promptly. "They're almost a day ahead of us. Right now, they're probably just getting up."

"Not unless you live on a kibbutz," said Mitch's father. "If you live on a kibbutz you have to get up very early in the morning to do the work on the farm."

"Everybody gets up early on a kibbutz," his mother said. "That's the way they do things there. They get up at the same time and go to sleep at the same time. They share all the work and take turns doing the least desirable jobs. In Israel, everyone feels responsible for each other."

"We all have responsibility for each other," his father said loudly and emphatically. "No matter who we are or where we live or how much or little we have or how smart or dumb we are, all human beings have responsibility for each other. That's a fact of life."

Whenever his father started talking about having responsibility, he always got to the newspaper glued to the dining room table. Mitch stood up.

He walked out of the room and clumped down the stairs. No one even noticed.

The basement had been finished off into two bedrooms. His was the one on the end. It was behind the furnace and had only one high skinny window in it. To open, the window lifted up. Through it Mitch could see the scuffed-up grass in the backyard, and the slat fence which surrounded the house. Originally, his bedroom had been the place where the coal was kept before the furnace had been converted to oil. In the winter, Mitch could lie on his bed and hear the stomach of the furnace rumbling. It was a comfortable sound; he was used to it.

Mitch flopped down on his bed. He had already pulled out most of the stuff that had been stuck away in his closet. Everything was in piles on the floor. The only things left hanging in the closet were the clothes that he was supposed to put into one bag. He raised his head to make sure that his sleeping bag was still there in the middle of his floor, and his backpack with it.

He heard his cousin Bernie amble down the steps. Bernie slept in the recreation room at the bottom of the stairs, but he kept on coming down the hall. Mitch didn't hear any knock. The door bounced open and Bernie came in.

Mitch looked at his cousin suspiciously. Bernie was as tall as Mitch's father but stringier. He didn't

look like a brain. That's what Mitch's father called him — the brain. He looked like he was always trying to prove he knew everything and wasn't afraid of anything.

Bernie's brief glance took in the stuff all over the floor. "Looks like you could use a little direction here."

"No, thank you," said Mitch.

"You won't be able to take all this stuff, you know."

Mitch didn't answer.

"One thing you can't take for sure is that bird's nest."

Mitch had almost forgotten about the bird's nest. He had found it once on a hike with Jeff. It had been sitting up there on his top shelf over his books ever since.

"If I go, it goes," he said without hesitation.

Bernie gazed at him consideringly. Mitch stared back stonily.

Bernie shrugged. Mitch lay back and listened as Bernie sang his way back down the hallway to his own room. The song he was singing was "Hatikvah" — off-key.

Mitch heard the basement door opening again and his mother's steps as she came down.

"*Lila tov!*" she said cheerily, sticking her head into his room.

He looked at her blankly.

"That's good night," she said. "In Hebrew. Everybody in Israel speaks Hebrew."

"*Lila tov!*" shouted Bernie.

"Good night," mumbled Mitch.

His mother stood there in the bedroom doorway looking at him. "You'll see," she said. "Everything will be just wonderful in Israel."

"I'm not going," he muttered, and pulled up the blanket.

"Some sense of humor," she said, and went out.

He lay back in bed and closed his eyes. A little later he heard the telephone ringing and the crisp edge of his father's voice. Like a salty cracker. The voices from upstairs began to fall dimly on his ears, like the flow of a distant waterfall.

After a little while, Mitch heard his father talking with his cousin Bernie. Mitch turned his face to the wall.

The teakettle started making its crazy whistle. The hallway light blinked. He heard the bathroom-door lock click. Someone was gargling. Pretty soon he heard the click again. He thought he smelled his mother's hair spray. And after that he must have been asleep because when he woke it was four o'clock in the morning.

Mitch got out of bed slowly. He dressed with deliberate care, zipped up his ski jacket, and opened the window. The sky was smoke gray, like a campfire before it bursts into flame. Mitch pushed his sleeping bag and backpack through the window and climbed out.

He crawled back in again to write the note and left it on his bed.

"I'm not going," it said. "You can't make me if I don't want to."

chapter 2

D<small>ARN PHONE</small>!" muttered Mitch's father as he pulled his head out from under the sink where he was trying to patch a pipe that had begun to leak. He had started to work on it right after dinner. You don't walk out of a house and leave strangers with a leaking sink.

"Can you get it?" His wife's voice was muffled. Her head was in the linen closet. She was leaving the shelves lined with fresh paper.

"Got it," he said as he answered the clamoring ring.

"Berson here!" he barked into the mouthpiece.

"Is Mitch there?" It was a scratchy voice. That would be Jeff. The scrape of Jeff's voice always annoyed him.

"He's asleep!" he said crisply. "Went to bed an hour ago."

"Oh." The boy seemed to hesitate. "Maybe you'd better give him a message."

Mr. Berson glanced at his wrist watch and set the telephone earpiece on his shoulder while he pulled at the memo pad. "Remember to pack moth balls," it said. That made him grin. And "Joe's

11

tooth." He wondered what about Joe's tooth. Had his wife intended to bronze it like the boy's first baby shoes and take it with them, or was that just an old reminder to record the day? He found a clean page. "Shoot!" he said.

"It's about the hike," said Jeff. "Tell him it's all off. I can't go."

"Hike? What hike!"

The voice at the other end seemed far away and polite. "Maybe he mentioned it and you forgot. Just tell him that I won't be going. I'm going to Washington, D.C., with my father. It just came up."

"Look," said Mr. Berson, not even trying to make any sense out of it. "In case Mitch forgot to inform you, we're packing up to go to Israel. He won't have time to go on any hike this weekend. So it's off all right. He's got a lot of things to do before our plane leaves Tuesday morning."

There was a dead silence at the other end.

"You hear me?"

"Yes, sir, I hear you."

Suddenly the thought of how near to Israel he was gave Frank Berson a peculiar wallop. He took a long deep breath. "I'll tell you what I'll do," he said generously. "I'll remind him to wave as we fly by. Okay?"

"You don't have to," the boy reminded him gently. "I won't be here either."

Mr. Berson hung up the phone and finished checking through the memo pad. He tore off page after page, crumbling each in his hand after he scanned it, and tossed them into the wastepaper basket. "Crazy kid," he muttered when he thought about it. Traveling halfway around the world and doesn't even mention the fact to his friends. "I'll never understand kids," he called to Miriam.

"What?" His wife came in with the leftover part of the roll of shelf paper and stood there in the middle of the kitchen as if she didn't quite know what to do with it. She looked tired. Her new hairdo was covered carefully with a pink nylon net. He touched the back of his own neck where the hair had grown long, and grunted. His sideburns had grown thick, even though the hair on the top of his head was sparse. He touched his fingers to the thinning spot regretfully. When he was Mitch's age, his hair had been cut to a stubble. Crewcut, they called it. The style. He smoothed the strands hanging at the back of his neck and chuckled.

"What's so funny?" his wife asked.

"Hair," he said. "When it's in, I'm out."

She gave him an automatic smile but turned her attention to the framed picture on the kitchen wall. Mitch had painted it when he was younger. Airplanes flying across the sky. Though Mitch wouldn't admit they were airplanes.

Funny, he couldn't help thinking, that a little

kid could paint a picture that looked like airplanes to everybody and never even know it. Maybe it was even funnier that he had never even tried to paint anything else. Kept trying to make more airplanes. Always was a funny kid.

"It won't make much difference once we're in Israel," Miriam said, looking at his hair.

That was automatic too, he thought. *As soon as we get to Israel, when we're in Israel, after we start off for Israel.* Suddenly a lump, a stone of premonition, filled his throat. He shook himself suddenly.

Miriam looked at him questioningly.

"When we're in Israel," he said emphatically, "we won't have to look at those damn airplanes any longer."

"Yes, we will." Impulsively, his wife took the picture off the wall and set it on the counter. "We're going to take this with us."

Frank went back to his work under the sink. Miriam stood there in the middle of the kitchen looking around wistfully.

"I just wish he were a little more excited about it."

"Who?" Frank wiped up a puddle of water that had dripped from the pipe under the sink to the floor.

"Mitch. He's been so quiet."

Frank gave a thought to his son. "Natural," he

said. "Bernie's the talkative one. Yack-yack-yack. Reminds me of my brother when he was a kid." He found himself staring at the wrench in his hand while he recalled moments he thought he had forgotten. His brother had been just like Bernie, he reflected. He saw the same wide-eyed look on Bernie's face, heard the same laugh whenever Bernie opened his mouth. Frank chortled softly. Bernie made him feel like a boy himself again.

"It worries me a little," Miriam said.

"What does?"

"Mitch."

"Nothing to worry about," Frank said emphatically. "Mitch is just a kid. Thinks he has to put on a big act. Probably inside he's jumpy with excitement." He touched his hand to his stomach. "Anyway that's the way I feel. Sort of jumpy."

"Me, too." Miriam glanced at the basement door. "I guess that's it." She sounded relieved.

"Mitch is just a kid," Frank said again, and set the wrench down. "I'll go down and say goodnight to him."

He went downstairs two steps at a time. Bernie's door was wide open; Frank looked in. Bernie's luggage was stacked in the corner. His collection of paperbacks lay in a neat pile on top. The convertible couch had been made into a bed. Bernie's shoes were on the floor at the foot. A chair held the clothes he had taken off.

"All set?"

"Just about." Bernie buttoned his pajama coat and got into bed. He grinned at his uncle. "Funny, my mother letting me go to Israel with you."

"Why funny?"

He made a face. "My mother has never let me go anywhere alone — not since my father died."

"I guess you can understand that."

He smiled as if he were old enough not to let it bother him at all. "She thinks she's got to decide everything for me — even what color socks I should wear."

"Well, Miriam usually buys my socks."

"Yeah, but that's different."

"Anyway, you are going to Israel with us."

"I guess I don't really believe it yet. I had this funny feeling today that the only place I'll be going is right back home to my mother."

"Nonsense!" said Frank. "That's all settled. We're as good as there right now. And I'll tell you something else — it's a good thing for Mitch to have an older fellow like you around."

"I don't think he likes me. Not much anyway."

"Of course he likes you!" Frank said. "Why wouldn't he like you? He's just quiet, that's all. Takes him a while to warm up. Give him time, he'll like you all right. Anyway, he's just a kid."

"That's what my mother thinks I am," Bernie said.

16

Frank laughed companionably with him. He closed Bernie's door behind him and moved on down the hallway to Mitch's door. It was closed. Frank opened it quietly and looked in. The light was off. The dim figure in the bed lay motionless, turned toward the wall. The closet door hung open; stuff was strewn all over the floor and loomed bulkily before him. The room was a holy mess. He shook his head as he carefully closed the door without going in.

The teakettle was whistling lustily when Frank returned to the kitchen. "Miriam?"

She came in wearing an old bathrobe she intended to leave for the Salvation Army or Goodwill pickup. "Thought you'd like a cup of tea," she said.

"Sounds good." He opened the cupboard and stared blankly at the empty shelves.

"The plastic cups." She pointed to the box on the counter.

He pulled the wrapping off the package and set out two cups. She placed a tea bag in each. He liked his tea strong. They sat at the kitchen table and watched the tea brew.

"You'll probably have to give a good-bye speech tomorrow night at Dorothy's."

"Who wants to listen to me?"

"Well, we're the guests of honor. They'll probably all bring poems and we'll have to read them

17

out loud. You'd better be ready to laugh," she warned him. "Even at the ones that don't rhyme!"

"Damned nuisance!"

"They're our friends. It was nice of Dorothy to invite the kids too. A big help."

He stared around at the empty cupboards. "Where are we going to eat Monday night?"

She laughed. "I thought you said it was all a damn nuisance."

"Not if the food's good."

"Well, as it happens, we're going to the Sterns.' "

"Who?"

"They just came back from a trip around the world, remember? They want to give us some traveling tips."

Frank groaned.

"The kids are invited with us too, and I've already told Joan that we won't be staying late. That we have to be up early Tuesday morning to get out to the airport on time."

The airport. Strangely, Frank felt another wallop of emotion inside him.

He reached across the table and put his arms around his wife's shoulders. "Miriam?" He pressed his face down on top of her head. She was always telling him that everything would be just fine.

"What?"

"Tell me everything will be just fine."

18

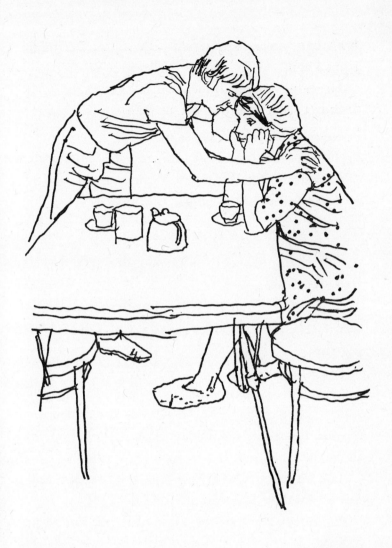

She giggled. "Everything will be just fine," she said obediently.

"Thanks." He picked up his cup of tea with

both hands and, leaning his elbows on the table, sipped at it.

He didn't bother to mention Jeff's telephone call. It didn't seem at all important then.

chapter 3

JEFF WAS LATE. He was usually late, Mitch reflected. Mitch unfastened his backpack and let it slide to the ground. He leaned against the signpost that said EDGEWICK ROAD. It had once been a logging road. It followed the middle fork of the Snoqualmie River, turning and winding twenty-six miles into the mountains.

Mitch peered at the smear of light on the horizon. He sat down on a scaly stump, waiting, watching the sunrise. First he could see the low hills all around. And soon behind them, higher hills. And as the sky turned lighter, higher peaks behind them.

He didn't mind waiting. He was in no particular hurry. He watched the misty vapor rising from the cool ground as the sun began to warm the air. It reminded him of a gently steaming teakettle.

The day stretched ahead like a carpet rolled out before him. He had this feeling — a peculiar sort of happiness. As if there were nothing more to worry about.

Mitch had ridden his bike out of the city and

left it at a gas station. He had stopped at a drive-in and eaten a breakfast of pancakes, then hitched a ride with a truck driver going east to cross the mountains. The driver had taken him through North Bend and dropped him at the turnoff to Edgewick Road.

Mitch took time to check his pack. Four sandwiches, two hard-boiled eggs, an apple, and a chocolate bar. Waterproof matches, a flashlight, and a pocketknife. A fishing line, some hooks, and a few sinkers. Rolled inside his sleeping bag were two cans of tomato soup, a spoon, and a frying pan. Everything was there he needed, he reflected — and he stood up to look up and down the highway. He began to wish that Jeff would show up, and turned his face to the early morning sunshine. He stretched and walked up and down a bit.

A camper truck turned onto the road. Then about six people riding motor scooters, half of them girls, were followed by another pickup-camper rig. A station wagon full of little kids in Boy Scout uniforms and a big black labrador went by, and then a girl on a horse. She didn't pay any attention to Mitch, just clopped right by. It was going to be a nice day. Lots of people would be hiking the trails. Or riding them. It was against the law to ride motor scooters on most national park reservation areas, but horses were okay. Personally he would much rather walk behind a motor scooter than a horse, he thought, and squinted at the sun.

A small pickup truck turned off the highway. Mitch stood alert for a moment. Not Jeff, he saw, and felt disappointment.

The truck stopped alongside him, backed up, and moved off the road onto the rocky shoulder. The driver got out, nodded to him, looked around, and then climbed in again.

"You waiting for somebody?" the man called out to him after a little while.

Mitch nodded.

"So am I." The man stepped down from his car. He had thinning gray hair and a smooth face. He wore a plaid woolen shirt, Levi's, and hiking boots. A cap, rolled up, was sticking out of his shirt pocket. He took it out, slapped it against his knee, and fitted it onto his head carefully.

They both turned their heads to the highway.

"This fellow I'm waiting for has been hiking with me for twenty years. We've been all over this area together. Guess we could write a book about it! Except neither of us is much of a hand at writing. We're figuring on going up to Dutch Miller Gap — you ever hiked there?"

Mitch shook his head. He had never been around here at all before. Jeff had this book on hikes. A hundred of them. They had taken two of them.

"Nice area," said the man. "Plenty of scenery.

Going up to Dutch Miller Gap you get almost everything — waterfalls, jungle forest, steep peaks. And even some subalpine country with heather and flowers. Pretty. At the gap there's a regular Japanese garden. Honest! All natural. A little meadowland and tiny waterfalls and pools, with rocks and ferns and dwarf trees."

He paused to shade his eyes from the sun and gazed down the highway. "We're figuring on camping there tonight. Fourteen miles, it is, for the round trip. Maybe even stop to fish a little somewhere."

"We're just going to hike around," said Mitch carefully. "We haven't picked any special place yet."

For some reason the man turned and looked at him thoughtfully. Mitch turned his head and kept his eyes on the passing cars.

"Ever been to Coppermouth?"

Mitch had never even heard of it.

"Hot springs," the man said. "Water comes right out of the rock at one hundred twenty-five degrees. Hot, all right. Not much of a hike though. It's probably not more than a mile or so from the spur at the end of the road. Fellow I knew used to live there. He built a couple of shacks there and an old building that used to be a hotel. Probably burned down by now. Everything round here gets burned down sooner or later. Campers sometimes; sometimes lightning. You got to be mighty careful in the forest. Most people aren't." He gave Mitch a hard look.

"I know," said Mitch quickly.

The fellow pulled at a weed, stuck it into his mouth, and started chewing. "Used to live about three miles from here when I was a kid. Knew all the rangers. Nice guys, those rangers." His jaws worked rapidly, and he spit out a mouthful of chewed-up weed. "Pshaw! Not what I thought it was. Thought maybe it was a licorice fern. The kind with a licorice taste."

His grimace turned to a grin. "Probably it wasn't a fern at all, and if it was, it was probably the wrong kind and the wrong time of year. My friend, he knows all about things like that."

Mitch looked at a clump of green growing at his elbow. Small shiny green leaves and tiny smooth round purple balls.

"Wild huckleberries," said his companion. "They're good to eat. The trails back there are full of them. It's the right time of the year for huckleberries. My wife makes pies out of them. Calls them blueberries." He laughed a little.

"They look like blueberries."

"Taste almost the same too," the man said, and stared out toward the highway. "Thought for a moment that was him coming. My partner. But guess not." He squinted at the sun.

"Haven't been to the Coppermouth myself for a long time. Not part of the forest reserve area, y'know. It's private property. Eighty acres of it almost, right in the middle of hundreds of acres of natural forest land owned by the government." He squatted Indian fashion, keeping his eye on the road as he talked. Mitch squatted too.

"Three guys prospecting for copper found the place — maybe seventy-five, maybe a hundred years ago. One of them homesteaded. He thought he'd make his fortune out of it. Figured he'd mine for copper, y'know. Well, he blasted a hole up in the rock wall, and blasted out a cavern about twenty feet deep. There was a copper vein there all right, but not much of one. He blasted loose the hot springs too. Steamy as you like it. Anyway, he never found any real mine."

Mitch glanced quickly at the highway and back to the old man's face again.

"Guess some big mining company is interested in the property now. Heard they had a crew up that area last year. Put up some shacks at the end of the spur, and put in a lot of equipment to see if there really was any copper around about there. They haven't been up there this summer though. Nobody much goes there. Not even hikers. I expect you'll find the hot springs still there."

Mitch nodded.

A big truck lumbered off the highway and

stopped on the shoulder. A white-haired man in a red plaid shirt got out. He pulled a pack after him, and waved as the truck moved off.

"Well," said Mitch's companion. "Here's where I shove off." He turned toward his own truck, and said companionably, "We could give you a lift to the spur if you want. That's where most of the trails start."

Mitch hesitated. He looked down the highway. It was already bright morning. "Maybe I will." He looked around vaguely. "I guess I'd better leave a message in case my friend comes." He began digging into his pockets.

"Here," said the second man. It was the first word he had said. He handed Mitch a paper plate. "Best thing for messages," he said. He sounded as if he were used to giving orders.

Mitch borrowed his pencil too. He wrote *Jeff* on the paper plate and a wiggly arrow pointing up. He stuck the plate on a nail on the signpost and hurried to climb into the truck with the waiting men.

"It's going to be a nice day," the driver said affably. The other grunted and said nothing at all.

He'd go to the end of the road, Mitch decided. He might as well go to the end of the road and wait for Jeff there.

The truck started up.

Mitch leaned forward and peered through the dusty window at the narrow road ahead.

chapter 4

F<small>RANK</small> B<small>ERSON</small> <small>FELT</small> the day beginning even before he opened his eyes. He sniffed the fresh morning air, flung the cover back, and lay there stretching and taking long, deep breaths. The smell of coffee came from the kitchen. He raised himself up briskly and got up smiling.

A day just beginning with the hours full on ahead always made him feel cheerful. He marshaled the things he wanted to do that day in his mind as he dressed. There was never time enough, he thought. A day was like a satchel — empty in the morning, brim full by night. And always at the end were those things left over that he had not had time to fit in. He began to hurry.

Their tickets to Israel were in the new wallet his fellow workers had given him on his last day. He opened the top drawer to look at it now. He opened it and looked at their tickets and passports, which he had placed inside, and closed it feeling a peculiar joy. They were practically there.

The telephone rang when he was still in the bathroom. He stopped shaving to listen. It was Louise.

He went on with his shaving. He could always tell when Louise called by the careful way Miriam talked into the telephone. Louise was his sister-in-law, Bernie's mother.

"I bet she asked you whether Bernie remembered to take his vitamins," Frank said when he came into the kitchen. Joe lunged at his leg, and he picked the boy up and placed him in his high-chair.

Miriam giggled. "As a matter of fact, she did."

"Beats me that Bernie isn't afraid of his own shadow, the way she's hovered over him since he was two years old." He thought of his last evening's talk with Bernie. "Do you know that his mother wouldn't even let him walk to school alone? She took him in the car every day. She wouldn't let him have a bike until he was ten years old; he never even had a pair of skates, and when all the other kids were joining the Little League, he was still swinging a yo-yo!"

Miriam smiled. "He's not a bit like Louise."

"Matter of fact, he's just like his father." Frank thought of his brother Bob. "You know, he even laughs like his father. It used to tickle me the way Bob laughed. We used to go to the movies and sit there in the balcony, and every time Bob laughed, the whole house would begin."

"What was his laugh like?"

"Just like Bernie's."

Miriam looked puzzled. "I guess I've never noticed."

"Something else he used to do, too. Sing. He had a pretty good voice and every once in a while in the middle of the night, he'd just open up and sing. Darndest thing. Wake up the whole house. Made our mother mad as hops."

"Heavens! I'm glad Bernie doesn't do that!"

"Same kind of voice," Frank said, feeling pleased that he had recalled that.

Miriam threw him an amused glance. "Bernie can't sing a note in tune. He's got a tin ear. Just like you."

Frank grinned. "Maybe that's why it sounds okay to me."

Miriam laughed too.

"Anyway it's nice having him around. Reminds me of his father."

"I'd suggest you stop calling him Bob and stick to Bernie. He doesn't seem to like it."

Frank looked at her in surprise. "Do I do that?"

"All the time."

Frank scratched delicately at his chin. "I never noticed I do that," he said.

For no reason that Frank could see, Miriam leaned over and kissed him.

"Good morning," said Bernie. His hair was neat, long but not too long. Curly. Like Bob's.

"Your mother called," Frank informed him.

"I took my vitamins," he said quickly. They all laughed.

"Where's Mitch?" Miriam said as she poured coffee for Frank.

"Maybe you'd better go down and wake him up, Bernie." Frank took a good sip of coffee. "Hot."

"He's already up," said Bernie. "I looked."

"He must have gotten up awfully early," Miriam said. "I was awake with Joe at six and I didn't hear him."

"I usually hear him," said Bernie. "He bangs things when he gets out of bed. He always leaves the toothpaste cap off, too."

"I guess he forgot to brush his teeth this morning," Miriam said. "He must have had something pretty important he wanted to do. I've had to drag him out of bed every morning this week."

"Probably took his bike over to the bike shop," Bernie suggested.

"He was supposed to do that yesterday," Miriam said. "We might as well go ahead with breakfast. He'll probably be here in a minute anyway."

A small tremor moved down Frank's arm and out to his fingers. The coffee in his cup slopped over.

Miriam looked at him in surprise.

Carefully Frank set down his cup. "Where did you say he said he was going?" he asked Bernie briskly.

"He didn't say," Bernie said. "I didn't see him."

"What's the matter?" said Miriam.

"Nothing," Frank said automatically. He took another sip of his coffee. Then he rose from the table and went downstairs.

The door to Mitch's room was half-open. He looked in. The covers had been pushed back on his bed. The same piles of junk seemed to be lying all over the room. The window was open.

Frank stepped over the bundles and boxes and closed it. He saw the piece of paper then, sticking out from under Mitch's pillow. He pulled it out. *I'm not going. You can't make me if I don't want to.*

Frank stared at the writing and remembered the phone call and Jeff's message. The hike. It was Mitch's way of telling him that he was going on that hike, thought Frank. His surge of anger was instant — not at himself for forgetting to give Jeff's message to Mitch — but at Mitch for not telling them about his plans to go hiking. His anger was justified, he told himself. He folded the paper and put it into his pocket. "Crazy irresponsible kid," he muttered, and moved slowly back down the hallway and up the stairs.

"He went on a hike," Frank told them, and poured himself another cup of coffee.

"Today!"

"I suppose it was my fault." He frowned. "I forgot to tell him that it was called off."

Miriam stood looking at him a moment in surprise.

"Telephone call," he explained. "Last night. He was supposed to meet the kid — Jeff. I don't know where they were going. To the mountains, I guess. He'll probably be back soon's he finds out that Jeff isn't going."

"He didn't tell me he was going on a hike," Miriam said. "I wonder why he didn't think to tell me."

Frank touched the fold of paper in his pocket. "Well, as a matter of fact . . ." he began.

"Hey!" shouted Bernie. "Who left the water running in the bathroom?"

Frank pushed the paper further into his pocket and strode down the hall. "Water?" He pushed open the bathroom door. Miriam was right behind him. The floor was covered with water.

"It's not the water faucet," Miriam said.

Frank moved quickly to the closet next to the bathroom. He opened the door, reached behind the water heater, and turned the handle. The sound of the flow stopped.

"The water heater," he said. "Busted."

"Oh for heaven's sake! How are we to get a plumber today?" said Miriam. "It's Saturday."

"A plumber can't do anything about fixing a busted water heater," Frank told her. "All he can do is put in a new one."

"Well, we'd better put one in then. And right away." She began to pull out old towels and mop at the floor. "Bernie," she called, "will you bring up the big pail that's downstairs behind the furnace? And there's an old string mop there too."

Then she stood there with her hands on her hips and began to laugh. "Wouldn't you just know it," she said. "Just when we're getting ready to go away."

"Let's just be thankful it's not worse," Frank said.

"Well, I can't think of anything worse happening. Not right this minute anyway." She swabbed at the wet floor with the mop Bernie handed her.

Frank stood there with his hands in his pockets. His fingers touched the crushed paper of Mitch's note. Mitch would be back before lunch, he told himself.

He walked past the scarred dining room table. Just seeing it always set his anger boiling. "Darn kid!" he began to mutter.

"What?" Miriam's voice came from the bathroom.

Frank raised his voice. "Mitch! The trouble with him is he doesn't know what responsibility means."

"He'll probably be back before lunch," she said.

Frank went into the kitchen and started looking through the yellow section of the telephone book. P for plumbers.

chapter 5

THE SMALL TRUCK lunged forward. The three passengers bounced and jostled on the narrow seat. Mitch peered through the front window. The road ran ahead of them in a zigzag course. The truck hurtled along, twisting and turning, like a quarterback on a school team. Rocks jumped at them from the roadway. Mitch heard the sound of small stones falling away.

"Not much of a road." The driver sounded happy. "Nobody much uses it anymore."

"Used to," said the second man. "Big logging operation around here once. Most of what we see now is second growth."

The truck jounced, a rock flew up and struck its underside. Mitch's head bumped the top of the cab.

"One big chuckhole," said the driver calmly.

They slowed down at a signpost. A fork in the road ahead. Straight ahead Camp Brown, 9 miles; the Taylor River Campground, 10. To the left Granite Lakes 5 miles, and Mt. Defiance Trail 6 miles. They went straight ahead.

YOUR CAMPFIRE reminded the next sign. NEVER LEAVE UNATTENDED. MAKE SURE IT IS OUT.

Thin trees leaned toward them from both sides, standing close together. Their branches stretched like arms across the narrow road, making an archway of trees.

"Pretty," said the driver.

"That's right," said the other. "Pretty."

Like going through a tunnel, thought Mitch.

Then they were out of it. They crossed a wooden bridge flung over a stream. Mountain peaks sprang up all around. They saw a lace curtain of falling white water hanging on a nearby mountainside.

The men were both silent. You didn't need to talk, thought Mitch.

"We must have passed Preacher Mountain," said one of them. "And Garfield."

"We ought to be able to see them all today." The driver ducked his head to look out. "We should be able to see Iron Cap, and Red Mountain, and maybe even Chimney Rock."

They passed a sign that said WISE CREEK, and then the road was lined with old vine maple trees. Green-gray beards hung from the high branches.

"Lichens," said the man at Mitch's side.

"Rained all over here yesterday."

"That's so."

"Remember to bring your rain gear?"

A grunt was the answer.

"We're going to need it."

"Maybe."

They passed a camper rig with a motorcycle in a trailer behind it.

"Probably run into plenty of campers," the driver said stolidly. "Fishermen, too. Probably see more damn scooter riders."

"Can't stand them," said the driver. "Never could, never will."

"An abomination," agreed the other.

"Pretty soon there won't be any wilderness area left at all. What with campers burning up the forest, and scooters tearing up the trails, and loggers cleaning off the hills."

The road turned sharply, and the driver swerved to follow it.

"You'd better stop talking and start driving," the man next to Mitch advised drily.

"If you don't shut up, I'll dump you out here and let you walk it."

The middle man grinned. "I got good hiking shoes," he said. "Plenty of wild huckleberries and salal to eat. Some good fish in the stream. I guess I'd make out all right. Might even enjoy being alone."

The driver grunted and kept his mouth closed and his eyes on the road ahead. He began honking as they made the next curve.

"Hairpin," said his friend.

"No it isn't! It's an S," the driver announced victoriously as he turned sharply the other way.

He slowed down to cross a wooden plank bridge. Mitch listened to the clunking sound of the thick planks and the roar of tumbling water beneath them. Beyond, a red strip of cloth was tied to a tree and beyond that someone else had posted a message on a paper plate. The trees were denser here — vine maples, firs, hemlocks, Western red alders — he couldn't name them all.

The driver peered into the forest glen on his side of the road. They rattled past an old carved signpost and took a left turn.

"Whoa!" shouted his companion. "You're going the wrong way."

The driver braked to a stop, opened the door, and, leaning out, backed the truck up to the point where he could see the signpost. He studied it carefully.

"That way's Otter Slide Falls," his friend said curtly.

The driver swung the truck the other way and went bouncing down the narrow road. On his friend's face was a contented smile.

"What you grinning about?" the driver said with a sour look.

"Couldn't get along without me, that's what,"

his friend answered. "You know it and I know it, and this young fellow here knows it too. Isn't that so?" he appealed to Mitch.

Mitch pretended he was staring out the window. "It's a bad road," he said carefully.

The driver poked at the man next to him gleefully, and laughed. "You're not going to get him to say anything against me. He knows who's driving this rig."

Mitch continued to stare straight ahead. A large bird flapped across the road in front of them. The man next to him turned and tried to catch another sight of it through the rear window.

"It was a duck," Mitch said.

"What?"

"A duck."

"Maybe."

"I had a duck once. Used to cross the street in front of our car just like that."

"What happened to it?"

"Well, one day it crossed the street in front of our car just like that."

The men laughed.

"I tried to draw a picture of it once. I figured I'd make it fly across the sky. You know, in formation with a lot of other ducks."

"Seen them do that."

"My mother framed it."

"Must have been pretty good ducks."

"My mother and father thought they were airplanes."

Abruptly the truck came to a stop. They had
come to a spur in the road. A red-earth truck trail

led off from the main roadway. A cable stretched across it barring any vehicles from turning down. A small dusty car was parked there.

"That's it," said the driver. He leaned over and flipped up the door handle. The door fell open.

"All you got to do is follow that road, past the miners' shacks, across the river, and there's a trail there that'll get you to Coppermouth. It's nice and easy."

Automatically, Mitch got out.

"If you're still about in a couple of days, we'll give you a ride back," said the other one.

"Thanks," said Mitch.

The driver leaned over his companion. "You'll probably be cutting right across the Cascade Crest Trail," he hollered. "It goes all the way down to Mexico, or up to Canada, headed the other way."

Mitch followed the direction of his waving hand. He heard the car door slam shut behind him, and when he turned again, the dusty truck was bouncing off down the road.

chapter 6

"Look," said Frank into the telephone. "We need a sixty-gallon water tank. It would help a lot if you could pick one up and bring it out here and put it right in."

Miriam stood at his elbow. The telephone directory lay on the table open to the yellow section. They had almost reached the end of the column.

"Tell him we're going away," she reminded. "Tell him we can't go away and leave a busted water tank."

He waved her to silence.

The man on the other end cleared his throat. "Well, I'll tell you," he said, and paused. "It's pretty hard to pick up a water tank on Saturday. Lots of places closed all day Saturday, you know. Supply places that is. Might have to look around a bit."

"Yes, I know," said Frank. "But I figured that if I had to, I could save you some time by doing that myself."

"It couldn't wait until Monday, huh?"

"Ordinarily, yes," said Frank. "Any other time we could get along. But you see, we're getting the house ready for renters. We're figuring on catching a plane early Tuesday. But we've got a million things to do —"

"You got your water turned off."

"Right."

"Well, I'll tell you what I'll do. You go out and pick up a new tank and I'll try to come out and get it hooked up for you."

"You'll be here?"

"Sure thing. By three — well maybe four. Soon's I can get away. We've got my wife's relatives coming for dinner. But I'll get there all right. Anyway I'll try."

Frank hung up.

"He said he'd be here, didn't he?" Miriam asked. She was fixing something for Joe.

"He *said* he'd be here." He frowned at the open telephone book.

"If he said so, he will," she said. "Won't he?"

"Well, it was the way he said it."

"I'm sure Mr. — whatever his name is — will come." Her voice was light and confident.

Her excitement had even made her face look different.

He remembered when they were kids there was a game called "Going to Jerusalem." The fantasy was about to come true for both of them. They really were going to Jerusalem. He grinned at her, feeling like a kid again himself.

"Last fellow I called was —" He tried to recall. "Dobbs?"

"I think that was a Mr. Mullen you called."

"Mullen?" He looked at the numbers scratched all over the pad. "What number did I call?"

"Emerson something."

He looked at the pad. Emerson 8-6644 was a Mr. Osborne. They looked at each other for a second and both began to laugh.

"Oh for heaven's sake," she said helplessly. "We're acting like kids."

He closed the telephone book. "I'm sure whoever he is will come." Saying it out loud made it more convincing.

"I'm sure he will," she said.

He looked at the clock. "Where's Bernie?"

"Off somewhere. Saying good-bye to his friends." She glanced at the clock too. "Do you think Mitch will have sense enough to give up waiting for Jeff and come right home?"

"What else would he do?"

She turned on the water faucet. She turned it both ways before she said, "Oh darn! I forgot. The water's turned off."

The doorbell rang. Weakly. If he had time he'd try to fix that too, Frank reflected. Miriam had already gone to open it.

"It's the movers," she called to him.

"The movers?!" They weren't supposed to come

until everything had been packed.

The fellow stood there at the doorway with a pink slip in his hand and a grin on his face. "Special orders," he said glancing down at the slip. "Says here we have to pick the stuff up today."

"Just a minute!" Frank barked. He went to the telephone.

"Do no good," the fellow called calmly. "No one's in the office today."

"Now look here," Frank said loudly. "It was distinctly understood that you people would come as soon as possible after Tuesday."

The man studied the slip. "You're right," he said cheerfully. "That's what it says here — 'Soon as possible.' And here it's marked 'pickup for Saturday.' "

"Well, you'll just have to come back," Frank heard himself shouting.

The man shrugged. "Suit yourself," he said, turning away. "But it says here it's going by ship — and that ship will be steaming out of here early Monday."

Hastily Miriam said, "You can start in the kitchen. Everything that's going from there is already crated. There are two trunks in my bedroom practically full and one downstairs. I just have to take everything out of the drawers."

Slowly Frank got up. "I'd better go down and pack up Mitch's clothes."

"Don't put in anything you don't have to," she advised.

Frank stood in the doorway of Mitch's room and sourly regarded the muddle before him. Finally he just plunged in, dragged the trunk to the doorway, and began putting in whatever was closest. Sweaters, a pile of socks, shorts, and T-shirts. Mitch's good suit was hanging in the closet. Carefully, Frank folded it, laid it in, and took it out again. Mitch would be wearing that on the plane. A raincoat. Shoes. Where in the hell was the other one? He put it in anyway and then took it out and laid it on the chair to await its mate. He stood uncertainly before the shelf of books. Take them or leave them? Israel was full of books. He didn't even consider the bird's nest. What would be the use of taking a bird's nest? Mitch's camera, radio. He dropped them in on top of the clothes and stood looking around. Funny how little he knew about Mitch. He was not a saver, that he knew. No collections, no bottle caps, no butterflies with their wings pinned back. He regarded the posters on the walls. *ZZZZAp!* said one. That's all — just *ZZZZAp*. Another was a large picture of a cow with flowers growing in her stomach. *Summer is a cow*, it said. Frank scratched his head. It made no sense. "Crazy irresponsible kid," he muttered, pushing the trunk away from the door to get out.

The front door was open. "Mr. Berson?" It was a smiling voice.

"Right here!" said Frank. He came forward briskly.

"I'm Nat Everly from J. C. Real Estate. I have your lease here all ready to sign."

"What is it?" Miriam's voice came liltingly from the bedroom.

"The lease," Frank called. She came hurrying in.

"Well, it will be good to get that settled," she said happily.

They stood there in the hallway while Frank glanced through it carefully.

"It's the same as it was before," the salesman hinted smoothly. "Just exactly the same with the addition of the lessee's signature."

"I know," said Frank. But he kept it in his hands a few moments longer. His eyes read one paragraph and then skipped to another.

The said Lessor does hereby lease and demise unto the said Lessee those certain premises situated in the City of Seattle . . .

Said premises are accepted by Lessee in their present condition and shall be kept in good order, condition, and repair during the term of this lease.

"It's all in perfectly good order," the salesman assured. "All you have to do is sign." He took out a black ball-point pen from his pocket, uncapped it, and offered it to Miriam — like the President offering his arm to the First Lady.

She grasped it firmly. "Where do I sign?"

The real estate man extended his hand delicately, letting it hover over the neatly printed contract in Frank's hand. "May I?" he said.

"Oh, sure," said Frank, "sure." He allowed the man to grasp it.

"Right here, Mrs. Berson." He flipped the pages professionally. "And your husband's on the line under yours."

Carefully Frank guided the pen through the letters of his name.

"That's all there is to it!" said Mr. Everly.

Frank stood at the doorway and watched him drive off. He moved to one side to make room for the movers to carry out a barrel. It looked like they were almost through upstairs. Frank walked down the hall to Joe's bedroom. Joe was in his playpen. "Hi, kid," Frank said. Joe grinned, taking his plastic toy out of his mouth to do so. Miriam was backing out of the closet with an armload of stuff.

"What I'd better do is go downtown and pick up a new water heater," he said.

"Stop at the donut place and pick up some of the applesauce kind," she called after him. "Mitch likes the applesauce kind."

"The applesauce kind," he said with a nod.

When he got into the car, he took Mitch's note out of his pocket and looked at it thoughtfully.

chapter 7

AT THE END of the side road, Mitch came to a clearing. The miners' shacks were there, about a half-dozen of them. They were made of plywood with sheet metal for roofs. The windows were boarded up. Mitch walked around the blue barrels and old gas tanks which lay about. A faded sign tacked on the largest shack said BEWARE OF THE DOG, and another, NO TRESPASSING. Mitch went past them, down to the river.

The river was wide and shallow and swift-running. A huge cedar log lay across it for a bridge. Some planks had been nailed onto the log to make walking across easier, and a wire rope stretched above it to give a handhold.

Mountain water was pure water, good to drink. Mitch scooped up a palmful. It tasted different from the water that came out of the tap at home. Colder, anyway.

He adjusted his backpack and walked halfway across the log bridge. Standing over the middle of the river, Mitch listened to the rush of water. Like water pouring into a bathtub. He stuck his fingers into his ears but the sound still rushed through. Loud.

He watched the water coming down from upstream. It ran hurriedly, pushing and rolling. It smacked up against the larger rocks humping up in the middle of the riverbed, splashing and going around both sides. It slapped at the small rocks, running over their smooth surfaces, kicking white foam. It speeded along, falling over itself again and again. It elbowed logs and branches in its way and shoved them aside, or picked them up and carried them along, to dump them farther downriver.

Staring at the moving water, Mitch began to feel as if he were moving too. It was like being on a train. The train going one way, and the landscape fleeing in the opposite direction. Jeff didn't like riding on trains, Mitch reflected. Jeff said it made him dizzy. The dizziness suddenly seemed real to Mitch too. Hastily he looked away from the moving water. He grabbed a firm hold of the wire railing and moved onto the other bank.

Three middle-aged ladies were sitting there. Just sitting on an old log. They all wore hiking pants and hiking shoes and had sweaters tied around their middles.

"Nice morning," one said with a nod and a smile.

Mitch nodded too and went quickly on.

He scrambled up a small rise, and came onto

a narrow forest trail. In a few moments the river sounds were gone.

Around him rose trees of Douglas fir, hemlock and spruce. Their thick green branches were as good as mufflers for noises.

He figured that the spongy mosses growing on tree trunks and branches and twigs and rocks, and on the ground and even on old stumps and fallen logs, helped too. So did the clumps of ferns that seemed to be growing everywhere.

Some fern fronds looked like swords; others reminded him of deer antlers. Some ferns were so tiny and delicate that their spines were only shiny black lines. A little farther on, Mitch saw ferns high as fences.

The trail below his feet was thick with dried brown needles. Mitch heard no sound from his own footsteps.

Above a bird whistled. Ahead he saw a branch snap and fall from a tree. He felt a cone drop on his head.

Mitch looked up. Long grayish green banners hung from some trees. "Lichens," he said, feeling pleased with himself. Fastened on other trees he saw liverworts. He looked up at bracket fungus seemingly hinged on the side of a tree trunk. It stuck out like a strangely placed seashell. One was on the ground. He picked it up. This one looked as soft and fleshy as a mushroom, but it felt firm and hard. He tossed it away.

He went on. Wild huckleberry bushes crowded alongside the trail before him. Their berries glistened, hiding themselves in thick clusters of leaves.

Mitch loosened his pack and set it down. He picked a handful of huckleberries and sat down on a mossy log. It was nice, he thought. Quiet. He didn't mind the silence. He ate the berries thinking about nothing. The sun poked fingers of light into the bowl of the forest. Everything was green. Warm yellow greens and cool green greens. He could feel the coolness right through the seat of his pants.

Mitch rose hastily and felt behind him. His pants were wet.

Mitch turned quickly around and put the flat of his hand down on the thick cushion of moss on which he had been sitting. It felt like a sponge. He pressed gently. Water oozed out.

Jeff would have laughed, thought Mitch. He would have folded over and laughed his head off. Mitch made a face. Nothing very funny about feeling your pants all wet.

He hoisted his pack onto his back again, frowned at the moss all around him, and walked on.

The trail turned and twisted, grew rocky, and at one point seemed to stop altogether. Mitch crawled over a fallen tree and found the trail there on the other side.

He came to a cross trail. A carved-out sign said CASCADE CREST TRAIL, and another with an arrow read HOTSPRINGS.

The fellow who had given him a ride had called it Coppermouth. Mitch followed the arrow. The trail widened and began to rise. Far ahead of him he saw the steep, pitched roof line of an old building, and off the trail close-by, two small shingled cabins. The doors stood wide open. Blackened circles of campfires guarded each door and discarded tin cans formed a crusty mound between them.

Mitch slipped out of his pack.

"You figure on moving in?" a sleepy voice asked.

Mitch jerked around. In the dark interior of one of the cabins lay a boy about his own age. Only his head emerged from his sleeping bag. His hair was long. There were whiskers of hair on his chin. His cheeks were red and his eyes blinked with sleep.

Mitch let out his breath slowly. "I might."

The boy yawned loudly, sat up, and stretched. He wore a purple shirt, the sleeves cut off at the elbows. A leather string hung around his neck, and from it dangled a can opener. "Well, I won't charge you anything. But it's against the rules."

"Thanks," said Mitch drily. He undid his pack, sat down, and began to eat his peanut butter sandwich.

chapter 8

I MADE SOME peanut butter sandwiches," Miriam called out to Frank.

"Mitch back yet?" He closed the kitchen door behind him.

She shook her head. "Imagine him going off like that and leaving everything sitting around his room. Not even finishing his packing. Do you know I found some of his dirty socks in his wastebasket. His wastebasket!"

"He's just a kid," Frank said. "In a hurry. Probably figured that if he stopped to ask us, we'd say no. So he just took off."

"He didn't have to ask," Miriam said sharply. "He knew what the answer would be." She looked at the clock. "And he'd better darn well hurry and get home. He's quite old enough to have taken the responsibility of packing up his own things."

"Maybe he figured on asking Bernie to help him." Frank thought of Bernie's admirably neat ways.

His wife looked at him oddly, he thought, and then he decided he had imagined it. "I got the water heater."

"Louise called. Twice."

For some reason, Frank felt a stirring of annoyance. "I wish Louise would stop treating Bernie like a baby. He's not a kid anymore. He's sixteen. Old enough to be respected."

"Well, he is her only child. It's understandable that she should worry about him."

"It's a wonder to me he isn't scared of his own shadow. She's always reminding him to be careful."

Miriam laughed. "Poor Louise. He scares her half to death most of the time."

Frank helped himself to a sandwich. He didn't like peanut butter much. "If Bernie's father were alive . . ."

"Did you get the water heater?"

Frank grinned at her. He understood Miriam pretty well, he reflected. She had a habit of making a quick change of subject when she didn't agree with him. Miriam didn't like arguments. Mitch was like her in that, he reflected. Did things the quiet way. Stubborn, but quiet. He stared for a moment at the full plate of sandwiches.

"I made a lot," she said. "Mitch will probably be coming home pretty hungry."

"He sure will be," he said loudly. He finished his lunch and went out to unload the water heater.

chapter 9

"Hardly anybody comes up here anymore," Charles said. "Not regular hikers, if you know what I mean. It's private property. Every once in a while one of the owners shows up and puts up a NO TRESPASSING sign."

Charles sat cross-legged on the ground before the black circle of ashes ringed by rocks. His lunch had been a can of beans brought out from inside the cabin. He had used the can opener hanging on the string around his neck to break into it and bend back the jagged lid. But he hadn't bothered to light a fire. He had eaten his beans cold, using a forked twig for a spoon.

Mitch didn't remember seeing any NO TRESPASSING sign. He looked at the pile of empty tin cans at the corner of the cabin, at the ash-filled fire pit, and swept his eyes over the cabin. Both roof and sides were made of thick cedar shingles. The kind that had been split by hand. The door was in the middle of the front wall and there was a window on each side. No glass. Someone, maybe Charles, had tacked up pieces of clear plastic. Inside the cabin was a cupboard built on one wall. There were the remains of an old potbellied stove standing against the other wall. A window had been cut into the back wall. The sun pierced through the stretched plastic and made a beam of light on the splintered plank floor.

"Not bad accommodations," Charles said. "Plenty of hot water." He grinned, and bent his head toward the other small cabin.

"It's full of old iron springs and junk and stuff. Someone must have built a fire right in the middle of the floor once. There's a big hole there."

Mitch looked up the trail to where the corner of a much larger structure showed through the trees.

"That's what used to be the hotel," said Charles. "There's a sort of trail near there. Goes about a half-mile up to the hot springs. Guests had to walk up to get their baths, I guess."

Mitch followed Charles up a pine-needle-covered pathway. The hotel stood in a clearing at the bend of a creek.

It was a large building, high as a barn. The gray weather-beaten structure was made of hand-hewn thick cedar planks set upright. The boards were a foot wide and some were twenty feet long. Slender peeled logs supported the shedlike slanted roof over the front porch. A second story could be seen rising behind it. The windows were tall and narrow. Each had eight square panes.

"Looks more like a barn than a hotel," said Mitch. He stepped carefully onto the old wooden planking of the porch. It was surprisingly firm under his feet. The old place had been built well, he thought. With a lot of care. "Loving care," Mitch's father would have said. Mitch would have substituted another phrase if he could have thought of one.

A handmade bench fitted below each of the two windows. The door was in between. It still swung open smoothly on its hinges.

"Supposed to have three floors," said Charles. "Only you can't prove it by me. Kind of spooky."

Mitch pushed the door open and peered in. It was a big room and seemed awash with trash. A broken stairway hung to the left. A big iron stove with a hanging stovepipe was near the wall at the right. The end of the pipe half missed the hole cut in the wall for it.

Tin cans, empty and rusted, surrounded the iron legs of the big stove. It was an old-fashioned range with grids on top and a hinged door to the firebox. The oven door was gone and a blackened inside gaped at them.

A table top lay on its side with no legs. It had been built like the benches outside. Thick cedar wood, smoothly planed. A broken chair lay on its back. Homemade too. Broken parts of a logger's saw stood about the room. An old iron bed and several flat broken springs were piled in one corner. A horse might have been stabled behind the stairs, for a piece of old harness lay there amid the other debris.

Mitch stepped back quickly. "It doesn't look like much. Not anymore, anyway."

"People had to hike in to get here," Charles said. "I mean really hike in. There wasn't any logging road then. I guess they had to use the old Red Mountain Trail. Must have hiked six miles anyway. Or maybe come on horseback."

Charles led the way around the hotel up a steeply ascending trail. Salal bushes swept their legs, and tree branches brushed their faces. The trail turned sharply, and all at once Mitch heard the roaring sound of water falling.

He looked down over the ledge and saw a pool of swirling water hundreds of feet below. Rising from it were moist canyon walls covered with moss and ferns. He stepped back quickly.

"It's a long way down," said Charles.

The trail became steeper. Bulbous roots formed a natural stepladder. Scrambling up after Charles, Mitch came suddenly to a more level, open space. They had reached a rock promontory above the top of the falls. Large rocks divided the waters of the creek. A cliff covered with hanging moss, lichens, and ferns walled in the far side of the creek. The other side of the promontory was thick with vine maples, ferns, and mosses and draped with shrubs. On this rock face loomed the Coppermouth, a yawning triangular opening. Steam floated out of the mouth of the cave.

"Wow!" said Mitch.

A large hollowed-out cedar-log tub stood close to the cave. Nearby were the remains of several other tubs.

Charles pulled at a piece of hose and placed one end of it into the hollow log tub. Water came through, hot and clear.

Charles pulled his T-shirt off over his head. "First, we sit in the tub, because it's not quite so hot. Then we dunk in the cold creek. Then we go into the cave. The water is hotter in there."

Mitch turned to look at the tumbling creek again. A shallow mountain pool had formed. Beyond it, great flat boulders filled the creek. They were covered with green stain and patches of moss. Mitch took off his shoes and walked to the end of the promontory. A handwritten sign had been stuck on a stick in the dirt there.

Rocks are slippery, it warned. *4 men, 1 child, and 1 dog have died here.*

chapter 10

IT WAS FOUR O'CLOCK when Frank looked at his watch. The next time he looked, it was twenty minutes past. The plumber wasn't coming. Somehow, Frank had known all along that he wouldn't.

He could hear Miriam talking over the telephone.

"We're waiting for Mitch," he heard Miriam say. "He isn't home yet."

Frank found himself standing, staring at the garden hose in his hands.

"Well, to tell you the truth, I don't know where he went. Hiking, I guess. He isn't too happy about leaving." Frank heard her giggle. "You mean Eunice. I never thought of Eunice as his girl friend. They just walk to school together. You know — kids." She listened. "Of course," she said. "I'm sure he will. He'll probably love it there. Anyway, we may be a little delayed coming tonight. Unless Mitch gets here in a hurry."

"Frank?" Miriam was calling him from the back door.

"Here." He rolled up the garden hose and plunked it into the wheelbarrow. The lawn mower, the hose, and the tools would be left in the garage for the renter. The lease had said so. The lease. He rolled the wheelbarrow into the garage.

"Is Mitch back yet?"

"Not yet," he said. He closed the garage door and walked wearily into the house.

"We're supposed to be at Dorothy's about five." She went to the front window and looked out. "It's getting late. He never gets home this late."

"I know," Frank said. "He was just going on a last hike. That's what I thought. Even when I read his note, that's all I thought."

She turned around so quickly that her elbow bumped against the window glass. She didn't even notice.

"What note?"

He pulled it out of his pocket, unfolded it, and smoothed it flat.

She looked at it, not saying anything. Not saying anything at all.

Frank looked out the window and saw Bernie strolling up the walk. Eunice was tagging after him. A skinny little girl with wispy hair that hung half over her face. She was laughing. Bernie was a charmer, just like his father, Frank thought. Then he felt his face twist, but not in response to the thought.

"He said he didn't want to go," Miriam said. Her voice was a hollow whisper. "He told us."

The telephone rang. Frank moved hurriedly across the room to answer it. The feeling of relief was already flooding over him when he picked up the telephone. "Mitch?" he barked into the telephone. Miriam's head was raised, listening. Her face still and expectant.

The voice came rushing at him.

He pressed the receiver against his chest. "It's Dorothy."

Miriam looked down at the creased paper, staring at it.

"She wants to talk to you."

Miriam shook her head. "Tell her we're not coming," she said dully.

For a moment Frank stared at the wall behind her head. He could see the outline of the picture that had hung there. The airplanes.

He spoke into the telephone carefully. "Look, Dorothy. Maybe you'd better not count on us."

He listened patiently to her reply.

"No, no one's sick. Well, it's Mitch."

He interrupted her. "He isn't home yet," he said. "Yes, we're worried about him." He looked at Mitch's mother and took a deep breath. "No, I don't know when he's coming home. We're not sure, but — well, it looks like he's run away."

chapter 11

"ONE DAY SOON I'm going to hike up to that ridge and go right over to Canada."

"Sounds good to me." Mitch leaned back against a log. He had heated his can of tomato soup by opening it and setting it on a piece of old grating laid over the fire. When it was empty he had tossed it over his shoulder onto the pile of cans.

"Or maybe Mexico."

A dull whirring sound stirred the forest.

"What's that?"

"Sounds like a helicopter."

"Oh." Mitch sat back again.

"Can't see us," said Charles. "We can see them but they can't see us. Trees too thick around here."

"Yeah." Mitch stared up through the trees until the sound faded away. "Did you ever notice how funny the sky looks from the forest?"

"How funny?" said Charles.

"Do you think that maybe the sky looks the same in Israel as it does from here?"

"Israel!"

"Yeah, Israel."

"Who cares how it looks in Israel?"

Mitch tossed a pine cone into the fire. "My father does, that's who."

Charles snorted. "I told my father that I was going to get out of the house and live by myself and he said I was just a stupid snotnose."

"At least he listened," said Mitch.

"Oh he listens all right. He listens and gets mad. No matter what I say — he gets mad."

"My father just acts like he knows everything, that's all. To hear him tell it, he knows it all."

"What gets me is my father's so dumb," Charles said. He sucked at the end of his twig spoon. "He's real Mickey Mouse, if you know what I mean."

"I know what you mean."

Charles grimaced. "Wall-to-wall desk and all that. With a vice president sign in gold right in the middle of it." He groaned.

"My father's never been vice president of anything except clubs and organizations. You name it, he's been vice president of it. He's got a pocket full of membership cards."

"You should see my dad's credit cards. His wallet is stuffed with them, if you know what I mean."

Mitch nodded. "That's what my mother gave me for my last birthday."

"What?"

"A membership card. To the National Geographic Society. It's the only regular membership card I have."

70

"I'm not a member of anything," Charles said proudly.

"Yes you are."

"No I'm not."

"You're a member of the human race."

Charles gave him a sour look. Then he uncapped a Coke bottle filled with water, thrust his head back, and took a large gulp.

"My father is kind of Mickey Mouse, too," Mitch said, and added a little self-consciously, "if you know what I mean."

"Yeah," said Charles.

"Like everything is labeled. Top, bottom. Up, down. Right, wrong."

"Hot, cold," said Charles.

Mitch grinned. "Off, on."

"High, low."

"In, out."

"Square, hip."

"Bad, good," said Mitch.

"That's what they keep telling us," Charles said. "If you know what I mean."

"What do you mean?"

Charles screwed up his face and gestured with both hands. "They don't give it to us straight." He frowned intently at the fire. "What I mean is — if *they* do it, well, it's okay. And if *we* do it, that's not okay. Bad trip, if you get what I mean."

Mitch stared at the small fire.

"That's all it is," said Charles. "Y'know?"

"Well, maybe," Mitch said doubtfully. "Of course I can see if it's not good for everybody, it's not good for anybody, no matter what anyone says."

"Right on!" Charles slapped him gleefully on the shoulder. "Good thinking." He grinned at Mitch. "That's what my father always says when someone agrees with him."

Mitch stretched his legs out toward the blaze and folded his arms comfortably over his stomach. He smiled companionably.

"You've got to look out for yourself! That's something else my father is always saying. If you don't look out for yourself, who's going to, you know?"

Mitch said, "My father thinks everybody is supposed to look out for everybody else. Like it's their responsibility or something."

"That's it!" shouted Charles, almost rolling into the fire in his excitement. "That's what they keep saying. It's nothing but a dirty communist plot!"

"I didn't know that."

"You got to believe it! That's what it is." He made a full gesture with both arms. "You see what I mean?"

Mitch wasn't sure, but he nodded wisely. "I see what you mean."

A figure emerged from the trail. A tall skinny figure with a blanket roll on his back. Charles stood up.

The man ambled forward, passed them with a nod, and went right on.

Charles stared at him a moment and then hollered, "Hey you!"

The man stopped and turned around amiably.

"You the guy that owns that funny skinny dog?"

"You mean Lady?"

"Well, dogs aren't allowed around here," Charles said loudly. Mitch looked at him in surprise.

The man remained standing uncertainly.

"You thinking of camping around here tonight?"

"Might." He shifted the roll on his back.

"Because if that's what you're thinking, I'll have to charge you a camping fee. This is private property, y'know."

The man scratched the back of his neck.

Charles scratched his neck too. "Don't like to take your dollar" — his voice suddenly turned soft and friendly — "but — well that's just the way it is."

"A dollar?" The man looked down at his feet. He wore tennis shoes. The laces had been broken and were knotted. There was a hole in the toe of one shoe.

"Or a candy bar," said Charles quickly. "You got a candy bar?"

They stood while the man stuck his hand in his pocket, pulled out a metal pipe, and carefully put it into another pocket. He searched through his jacket pockets and extracted a Hershey bar. He held it out.

Charles took it. "Okay," he said authoritatively. "But if you want to stay another night, you'll have to give me something else."

The fellow turned and went on toward the old hotel.

Charles came back to the small fire, unwrapping the chocolate bar as he walked. The firelight caught the gleam in his eyes.

"They're real dumb, some of those potheads," he said happily. "Almost as dumb as the rangers. Nobody ever asks anything."

Uneasily, Mitch kicked at the fire.

"When you're out on your own, first thing you've got to learn is be independent." He took a bite of the chocolate bar, wrapped the remainder up again and stuck it into his pocket. "You got to stand up for yourself."

"Sure," said Mitch. He began to spread out his sleeping bag within a circle of trees, kicking away the tiny clusters of cones. The trees grew close together here. They were tall and straight, with stringy gray bark. Some of it hung in long strips.

Mitch took off his shoes and crawled into his sack. He pulled the zipper up to his armpits, and lay there with his arms out. He reached out and picked up a twig, rolled and squeezed it between his fingers, and sniffed. He smelled a familiar fra-

grance. Like the cedar-lined closet at home. Like shingles and shakes. Like grapestakes, siding, fencing, fence posts. Like dugout canoes.

He took a deep breath and with half-closed eyes watched the shadows growing thicker around him.

He heard Charles laugh. "You should have seen my father last Saturday," he said. "I left my wallet somewhere. He gave me the keys to his car so I could go look for it. So I went. But I figured if somebody ever found anything they'd keep it, so I decided to just keep going."

"It's nice here," said Mitch.

"I'll probably just stay here awhile," said Charles.

"Maybe I will too," Mitch said. He turned on his side and then flopped over again on his back. He lay there with his eyes open. The night sucked up the light left under the trees, leaving blackness all around them. Mitch looked straight up to see the tips of the trees sharply outlined against the sky.

"It's still light up in the sky," he said.

"Black as hell down here." Charles's voice bounced out of the darkness.

"If it was hell it would have to be red or orange — like fire."

"Okay. Black as the grave, then."

Mitch shivered and closed his eyes. But that was no better. He opened them again, though there was almost no difference in what he could see. He tried closing his eyes tightly and saw little fireworks under his lids.

"Black as hell," he agreed.

Charles laughed sleepily. "Good night."

"Lila tov," Mitch said under his breath, and opened his eyes wide. He tried to make out the forms of the trees around him. He couldn't see them exactly but he felt them there, leaning against one another, their branches armlocked together, fencing him in. The darkness began to press against his eyeballs. Mitch shut his eyes.

The night felt soft. He could feel its blackness all about him. He kept his eyes closed and listened. Nothing. Even the sound of the waterfall had become part of the loud silence. Nothing. Nothing. More nothing.

The night neither hummed nor rasped. It didn't squeak or drip. There were no knockings, no stirrings, no footsteps, no rustlings, no hummings, no tinklings, no garglings. His eyes began to feel heavy. The ground underneath him was hard but it began to feel good. He began to feel as if he never wanted to get up. He heard Charles grinding his teeth. He felt the trees bending closer to him. He heard his mother going back up the stairs. Someone had left the light on in the hallway. He opened his eyes. It was morning.

chapter 12

"IT'S MORNING," Frank said. He watched the thin streak of light edging in under the window shade. Shiny. Like the blade of a knife.

Miriam turned and looked toward the window. "Anyway, it's not raining," she said. She must have been lying awake. As he had.

"You didn't sleep much."

"Neither did you."

"I know." She pushed the hair away from her face. "I guess he had to prove to us that we couldn't decide this for him. I guess he wanted to make us see that he wouldn't be treated like a child." Her mouth twisted. "I keep thinking about Mitch saying he wasn't going. I never paid any attention."

Uncomfortably, he raised his head and plunked it down on the pillow again. He hadn't paid any attention either.

"Why didn't he say something?" He let his anger rise. "If he thought he was so grown-up, why didn't he act grown-up! Running away. Only a kid thinks of running away."

"He did say something," Miriam pointed out.

She swallowed carefully. "He told us. He kept saying he wasn't going. We didn't even listen."

"Who didn't listen? I listened. I heard him all right. I just didn't think it meant anything."

"Well, now we know it meant something," Miriam said tiredly. She took a tissue from under her pillow and blew her nose.

"What time is it?" She looked at the clock — that is, she looked where the clock had been. She groped for her watch on the table by the bed, looked at it, and laid it down again. "Do you think they'd have heard anything yet?"

She meant the police. Frank had called the police last night. They had connected him with the juvenile division and asked for a description. They had asked for details — height, weight, color of eyes, color of hair and ski jacket. It embarrassed him that he didn't know some of it. Mitch was, well, Mitch. His son. He had never divided him up into sizes and colors.

His mother had known all of it, exactly. She even knew the color his jacket lining was — red — and that he was wearing white socks and his old tennis shoes, the ones she had already put into the discard box. She knew that he had taken his sleeping bag and two cans of tomato soup. Things like that.

They had asked him to list the places Mitch liked to go. Like the playground and the swimming pool.

They had asked for all Mitch's friends' names too. The only ones he could think of were Jeff and Eunice.

"It takes a little time to process," Frank told his wife. "They have to write up the information. Make copies. Send them to certain points. It's the regular routine, they said."

"Routine," she echoed grimly. "Not to us."

"They said they'd call us in the morning if they had anything for us."

"It's morning," Miriam said wearily. She pushed the covers back and placed her feet on the floor.

Frank got out of bed too. He began putting on his clothes. He needed a shave, but he remembered that there was no hot water.

"They said it would be a good idea to scout around myself a bit. You know — Volunteer Park, Golden Garden Beach, the Center, Alki Point. Places where kids hang out."

"All night?" she said with surprise.

"That's where a lot of them go, they said. Sleep anywhere. The police said they've been getting twenty to thirty calls a week on runaway boys."

"That's not the same," she said quickly. "Mitch went hiking."

"We don't really know," he reminded her. He had finally contacted Jeff's father by long distance at midnight. He had spoken to Jeff, too. They had not decided where they were going to hike, Jeff had said. Just where they were going to meet. Jeff didn't figure Mitch would start off on a hike without him. The police didn't think so either. Most likely he had come back. But had not gone home. It was summer; the parks were full of kids.

"Look," he said gently, "why don't you try to get some sleep?"

But Miriam was already getting dressed.

"Twenty to thirty," she said as she pulled a brush through her hair. "Where do they go to?"

"To their friends, some of them, the police woman said. Some stay out half the night and sneak back home. In the morning, the officer said, there they are asleep in their own beds."

Miriam put down the brush. "You don't think — "

"No," he said. "I thought of that; I've looked already." He pretended that was routine, too.

They had instant coffee, sitting together at the kitchen table.

"Maybe we'd better check with the police again," she said.

"They'll call us as soon as they have anything."

The sun streamed through the window. Bernie's door squeaked open. Joe began banging on the side of his crib. The telephone rang.

They both reached for it, quickly, together. But Miriam got it first.

"Hello?" The hopefulness was there in her voice.

He watched the expression fade from her face.

"It's Louise," she said, and handed the telephone to Bernie as he came into the kitchen.

She walked out of the kitchen toward Joe's room. Frank leaned against the counter, noting without thinking about it how reluctantly Bernie placed the telephone against his ear.

"Hello? Oh, hello, Mother. Oh sure. Sure, Mom. No, I won't forget. No, I'm fine. Really I am. Just fine."

Frank reached into his pocket, fingering his keys.

"All right," said Bernie, and handed him the telephone. "Mother wants to talk to you," Bernie said, and walked quickly out of the room.

"Hello, Louise." If his voice sounded crisper than usual, Louise didn't notice. He had decided he would not tell her yet that Mitch could not be found.

"Frank?" Louise as usual sounded anxious. "You're sure Bernie still wants to go with you?"

"He says he does," Frank said shortly.

"Well, I just wanted you to be sure to tell him that he doesn't have to if he doesn't want to. In case he's changed his mind, you know, and doesn't want to say anything."

"Look, Louise," Frank couldn't help saying. "Stop treating Bernie like a baby. He's not a kid anymore. He's sixteen."

"Just sixteen," Bernie's mother reminded him. "He's never been away from home, you know."

"I know," Frank said grimly.

Her voice quavered and then grew stronger with each word. "Maybe I should tell you the kinds of crazy things he's always doing. No sense. No caution."

Frank glanced at the place where the clock had hung on the wall. He stared at the blank spot and thought how bound man was by the hands of a timepiece.

"He'll be all right, Louise," he said. "Don't worry about him."

"Well, you tell him," she said, no less anxious. "You will, won't you?"

"I will." He hung up.

Miriam came into the kitchen carrying Joe. "You told her?"

"No."

She set Joe down into his highchair and opened the refrigerator door to get his milk. "What did Louise want?"

"She said to tell Bernie that he doesn't have to go if he doesn't want to."

His wife turned a startled face toward him.

He looked away.

The doorbell rang, loudly. Demanding. Bernie appeared and answered it.

"I'm here," they heard a hoarse voice say.

Frank's heart jumped. "Mitch!" he called loudly.

"It's me," said the strange voice. "Osborne, the plumber."

chapter 13

THERE'S THE AX behind you," Charles directed, with only one eye open. He lay there, still wrapped in his sleeping bag.

Mitch picked up the ax and began to hack at the limb of a small tree.

"Hey! What're you doing?" Charles's head was up, both eyes open, staring at him.

"Getting wood for a fire."

Charles flopped back again. "Dry wood," he said. "You've got to find some dry wood. Wood that's growing is green. It's got to be dry, real dry, to burn."

Mitch looked around. The forest floor was clean. No dead branches anywhere. Everything that had fallen to the ground had taken root.

"Just hack a board off the old hotel," Charles said from his sack.

"Doesn't it belong to someone?"

"Sure," said Charles. "Us."

Mitch moved on up the trail. A finger of smoke was coming out from the hole on the side of the hotel. The door was open. Mitch looked in. He

85

guessed the man was out looking around, too.

An old coffee tin of water was heating on the stove. There wasn't much of a flame under it. A chair leg stuck into the firebox burned lazily at one end. As he watched, it fell out and hit the floor, still burning. Mitch picked it up and shoved it in again. Then he went outside. There were no loose boards on the building. He walked all around it. It was built to last another hundred years, he reflected.

Coming around to the front again he regarded the two benches. The leg on one was splintered. He whacked at it with the ax and carried the pieces down to the campsite.

Charles was up, out of his sack, but he didn't offer to lend a hand. He sat there and gave orders. When the small hot fire was going within the circle of rocks, he went into the cabin and brought out two cans of beans.

"I've got plenty of beans." He pulled a carton out to the doorway. It was more than half full.

"You carry that all the way up here?"

Charles shook his head. "Not me. I got my own storeroom." He jerked his head in the direction of the miners' shacks. "Enough to last for a while, anyway."

"Until you get up on the Cascade Crest Trail."

"Until I get up on the Cascade Crest Trail," Charles repeated, but not very convincingly.

They ate their meal, Charles using a stick for a spoon again.

"Today is Sunday," Mitch said.

"Not to me." Charles twigged up the last of his beans.

"Why not?"

"It's not anything to me. It's just" — he made a vague gesture with his hands — "daytime, if you know what I mean. As far as I'm concerned it's got no name, no number, no nothing."

"You mean you don't care."

"That's near enough." He threw the empty cans over his shoulder.

"Even so, it's still Sunday," said Mitch.

Charles looked up at the sky. "Well, whatever it is, I've had enough of it." He stepped over the fire, pushed his legs into his sleeping bag, zipped it up, and pulled the flap over his head.

Mitch walked down the trail toward the river. He crossed the log bridge to the other side and sat on an oil barrel for a while. The skinny old dog he had seen the day before came ambling over the bridge and sat down next to him.

Mitch had to laugh. "Some watchdog," he said to the animal. He leaned down and scratched at its neck. The dog blinked, lifted its paw, and scratched at the same spot thoroughly. "Dumb dog," said Mitch.

Mitch went down to the water's edge and stuck

his face into the cold running water. The dog watched him curiously and stuck his nose in too. It must have been colder than he had thought. The dog looked up quickly in surprise, the water dripping from its face.

Mitch picked up a small stone and tossed it into the shallow water. The dog sprang forward and stood with his four feet immersed, looking as if he were surprised at the number of rocks covering the river bottom.

Mitch picked up a stick and tossed it in; the dog splashed forward, caught it, and brought it back.

Mitch flung it again and grinned as the dog leaped after it. The stick swirled downstream and the dog began to swim to get it.

"Here, fellow," Mitch called. "Come back, fellow."

The dog kept swimming against the current and stayed in one place. A drifting alder branch passed him right by.

Mitch stood up. He whistled at the dog. "Here, boy! Here, boy!" he called, and tried to whistle again.

Though the dog was still swimming, the current began to carry him the other way.

Mitch splashed into the water to get him. The dog caught on to a branch floating downstream, clutched it in his mouth, and with it became wedged between two rocks. Before Mitch had a chance to reach out to him, the dog had scrambled onto the rock, leaped slippingly to another, and with the branch still in his mouth had reached the other side.

The pounding in Mitch's chest subsided. "Good dog!" he shouted.

It was the wrong thing to do. He saw the dog pause, shake himself, turn around, and again plunge into the stream led by the sound of Mitch's voice.

"No!" shouted Mitch. "Stay there!"

He ran across the log bridge and flung himself onto the other bank. "Here, boy!" he shouted. "Here, boy. Here, boy."

The dog stopped uncertainly for a moment and then turned back. Mitch grabbed hold of his collar and pulled him out. "You stupid dog," he said. "You just plain stupid hound."

The animal sat blinking, then shook himself vigorously. He walked sedately back across the log bridge, jumped onto the opposite bank, and ran up the red-dirt road toward the logging spur.

Mitch sat down. He sat there for a little while by the side of the river until the shaking inside him had stopped. Then he walked slowly back along the trail to the Coppermouth.

chapter 14

IT WAS his third stop. Frank moved his car slowly around the boulevard looking for a parking spot. There was often a concert in Volunteer Park on Sunday afternoon.

He passed the ice cream wagon parked near the rose garden. He drove slowly past the entrance to the art museum. Marble statues of rams guarded the long, low building. Once he had snapped a good shot of Mitch sitting on one of the rams. That was a long time ago.

Frank saw an opening, and waited politely until a small car backed out. He pulled his car back a little to give the driver more room. Another little car pulled out from behind him and flashed right in. Helplessly, Frank sat there in the middle of the road, sodden under a wave of anger.

A young fellow backed out of the little car.

"Did we take your spot? Sorry!" he said blithely.

Two more kids piled out. A girl, or was it a boy? Another. Well, *he* was a boy all right. Girls didn't have beards. Not yet.

He moved the car forward, went around the boulevard again. He found a place finally, and slid in. He locked the car carefully. Absent-mindedly he found himself trying the door handles as if he had left something of value inside.

The sun was high; he squinted up at it. He passed the ice cream wagon and looked hurriedly at the line of people at the window. Lots of kids everywhere. He saw a slender figure and hurried toward it.

Not Mitch.

He stood still a moment scanning the entrance area. Moving slowly through the clusters of young people sitting on the wide steps, he turned around at the big doors of the entrance and quickly went back down. He crossed the street and walked through the park. He saw girls with hair hanging down to their waists and bare feet. Boys with long hair and bare chests.

A girl laughed at him. At him. He felt suddenly uncomfortable and didn't know why. He pushed his hair away from his neck and felt the thin spot on top. A boy, bare to his waist with a medallion on a chain hanging around his neck, looked at him with white teeth flashing. His hair ballooned around his face. "You looking for something, dad?"

Frank shook his head. Somebody, not something. He walked on. Not here. Not here. Not there. He made his way through the park, then got into his car again and drove out.

Alki Beach, Shilshole Bay, Golden Gardens. The sun went behind the clouds. It began to rain, lightly at first. The sun came out again. Then it poured.

Wearily he drove his car back up his own street. He found himself hurrying up the walk.

"You hear anything?" His hopeful voice preceded his body.

The answer was soft, almost voiceless. "No," said Mitch's mother. "Nothing at all."

chapter 15

I JUST COLLECTED the second night's rent," Charles said.

Mitch frowned. He had the fire blazing and poked at the edge with his foot.

Charles settled himself with his back against a log and reached into a pocket. He pulled out a twisted cigarette. It was filled with greenish tobacco. Charles licked one end, fingered it carefully, put the cigarette into his mouth, lit it, and sucked in. He passed it over to Mitch.

Mitch puffed at it. He swallowed some smoke and felt it in his throat. The smoke smelled a little like burning leaves. He passed the cigarette back.

A little earlier, Mitch had found some long thick boards piled up behind the second cabin, and had dragged them over to their fire ring. He got up now, and stuck an end of one into the small blaze. It was old and dry. He watched it catch and burn steadily.

"Springboard," said Charles. He gave Mitch another turn at the smoke.

"You mean this place had a swimming pool?"

Charles laughed. He laughed with great enjoyment as if Mitch had been very funny.

"A springboard is what the loggers used to stand on when they cut down one of the big firs or cedars. What they'd do was make a notch in the trunk several feet above the ground. Then they'd stick the end of the board in. It made a platform for them to stand on when they were sawing back and forth."

"Oh." Mitch pushed the board a little further into the fire. It seemed sort of funny to him too. He looked at Charles's face glowing white in the firelight and laughed along with him.

He thought of the chair leg falling out of the old stove up in the hotel, and the smoke coming out of the pipe right into the room. Just thinking about it made him laugh again. He took another turn at the smoke. The night began to fall around them and Mitch felt warm sitting in front of the fire.

And happy. He couldn't remember when he had ever felt so happy. There was nothing he had to do if he didn't want to. Nothing at all. Suddenly that seemed very important, very meaningful to him.

"Looks like it's going to rain," said Charles. He turned his face up to the sky.

"I don't care."

"If it rains really hard we can both sleep in the cabin, or else in the hotel."

Mitch thought of going up to the hotel to sleep. He remembered the holes in the floor, the sagging stairway, the stove with the broken chimney pipe. He grinned at Charles. "We'd have to sublease it."

Charles laughed some more too.

"Anyway it smells better out here," said Mitch.

"We'll get wet."

"We could go up to the hot-springs cave and steam out until the rain stops."

"Good idea."

"You got any brothers or sisters or cousins or anybody?" Mitch asked.

"Nah. None that count, if you know what I mean."

"What do you mean?"

"Well, I've got this one cousin who's looney, y'know. He's a preacher on Sundays and drives a taxi the rest of the week."

"That doesn't sound looney to me."

Charles grinned. "It would if you were my father."

Mitch nodded in quick appreciation. "I've got a brother. He's only a little kid. Still talks funny."

"What do you mean funny?"

"Like babies talk. Nobody but me can ever understand him. I can always tell what he means."

Charles hadn't stopped grinning. "How can you tell?"

"I don't know. I just do." He lost interest in the subject and gathered up a handful of pine needles. He sniffed the pungent odor deeply. "Green."

"What?"

"Everything smells green."

"I can't smell anything."

Mitch thrust the stuff under Charles's nose. Charles pushed it away.

"I guess I was born without a sense of smell."

"Oh. Well, that's no worse than having no sense of responsibility." The hard edge of his father's voice came to his ears. *He doesn't know what responsibility means!*

"What's the matter?"

"My father." Mitch mimicked his father's brittle tone: "Everybody has responsibility for everybody else."

Charles placed a friendly hand on Mitch's shoulder. "I feel for you, I mean I really feel for you."

"I don't let it bother me," Mitch said. He shrugged it off. "We've never seen things the same way."

"Well, it's not your problem then, you know what I mean?"

"You're right. It's not my problem," said Mitch, feeling happy about that.

Charles took the candy bar out of his pocket. He pulled back the torn paper wrapping, and put the whole piece that was there into his mouth.

"You're better off," he said with his mouth full.

Mitch peered at the stark roof line of the hotel through the trees.

"That way you don't have to worry about anyone but yourself," Charles said approvingly.

Mitch nodded. "It's the only way to get along in this world," Mitch said loudly.

"Right on!" said Charles.

Mitch felt good sitting in front of a fire, out in the middle of a forest, laughing. It seemed to Mitch to be the most pleasant thing he had ever done.

The rain began to get heavier and make splutters in the fire. The fire went out but Mitch didn't care, for they had moved inside and lay on the floor of the cabin. Wrapped in their sleeping bags they listened to the rain dropping on the thick shingles. *"Lila tov,"* Mitch sang to himself. *"Lila tov."* And he would have slept soundly if he hadn't been bothered by the smell of burning potatoes.

When he opened his eyes, the night was still black, and the sound of falling water was all around him. So was the smell of burnt potatoes. A bitter, acrid, wet smell. He sat up.

"Hey, Charles?"

No answer. He pulled his feet out of the sleeping bag and whacked at the mound next to him. Charles's sack was empty. Mitch opened the door of the cabin. The fire in the circle of rocks was a puddle of ashes. No potatoes.

Mitch zipped up his jacket and pulled the hood out from under his collar. He yanked the string tight under his chin and hurried up the trail toward the old hotel. He met Charles coming toward him. The water streamed off Charles's head, down his nose.

"Poof!" said Charles, making a circle with his hands. "The old place just went poof!"

Mitch gazed beyond him, smelling the caustic smell of burned cedar and wet ashes. He saw a column of smoke.

"Caught fire just like that," shouted Charles. "Nice and warm around here for a while, you know what I mean? Then it rained like blazes."

Mitch ran, stumbling up the trail. The man was just sitting there, squatting on his haunches. He held an old blanket around him. "You all right?" Mitch shouted.

The hotel was a burning black shell. The heat of it struck their faces. All at once it collapsed, a pile of blackened wood, sputtering in the rain.

The man turned a soot-streaked face to Mitch and waved his arms at him.

"I'm paying out no more rent," he hollered. "You tell him that, will you?"

Mitch took a long deep breath, and the bitter smell of smoking timber stung his throat. He covered his face with his arms. "You'd better get out of here," he shouted, and ran back to the cabin.

Charles was rolling up his sleeping bag. "I've found a good place. We'd better stay out of sight for the rest of the night in case the rangers come in, you know what I mean?"

Mitch picked up his sleeping bag. Charles kicked at the fire ring, skittering the rocks away.

"I'll leave the door open," said Mitch. "That way they'll think no one has been here."

"Nah," said Charles. "That way they'll know someone has been here for sure. Close it. Like it's been closed for a long time, you know what I mean?"

Mitch shut the door hard and followed Charles into the woods.

"We can see who comes and when they leave, you know what I mean?" Charles dumped his stuff behind a large fallen log, and crouched, listening.

"What do you hear?" Mitch whispered.

"Nothing." Charles stuck his feet into his sleeping bag and drew the upper part around his head. His face stuck out in the rain, sharp and bumpily white.

Mitch flung his sleeping bag down and crawled in. He leaned into the shelter of the log and pulled the sack up around his head. He closed his eyes, feeling the wet and the damp, but he fell asleep anyway.

He dreamed he was standing up to his waist in the river, throwing a stick for the dog to recover.

Only instead of the dog, he saw his father's shoe tossing in the middle of the stream. His father wouldn't go to Israel without his shoe. In his dream Mitch was going to reach out his hand and grab hold of the shoe. But he didn't, and suddenly it was gone. Mitch couldn't see it anywhere. The river splashed into his face.

Mitch opened his eyes. He was in his sleeping bag, huddled behind the big wet log. Rain was dripping down his nose and it was almost morning.

chapter 16

FRANK LAY in the gray place that was sleep. The early morning rain tapped at the bedroom window. It twitched at the blanket of his sleep. He stirred and muttered, clinging to the grayness, pulling it about him, wanting to hold it around him for a while yet. He hadn't slept much again.

From outside the bedroom door came the familiar sound of his young son. Incomprehensible.

"What did you say, Joe?" Miriam was talking loudly. "Say it again."

The bedroom door was partly open. The voices from the hall bombarded him.

Say it again. Say it again. Frank flung himself over, trying to hold on to sleep.

"What does he want?" he mumbled with his eyelids held shut. A grumble.

Miriam's voice spilled away from its tightly held motherliness and splashed anger over him. "I'm trying to find out what he wants!"

Frank made a desperate clutch after the escaping slumber. "Well, ask Mitch!" he shouted.

Then abruptly he was awake. Wide-awake. For a

moment he had forgotten that Mitch was not there. He opened his eyes and saw the expression on Miriam's face.

Quickly he pushed back the covers and got out of bed. "Here, I'll take care of him," he offered roughly.

Miriam turned her shoulder. She held on to Joe tightly. She would not look at Frank. "The coffee's on," she said.

Slowly Frank dressed, stopping often to rub his face with the palm of his hand. He had fallen asleep only moments before Joe awoke. When he looked into the mirror, his eyes appeared red-streaked, the lids puffy. Like a drinker who has been hitting the bottle. He gave a short laugh. Hitting the bottle — an odd expression. His reflection looked back, twisted. Sacked, like Rome. It was a humorless thought.

He moved slowly toward the smell of coffee.

chapter 17

Mitch wiped his arm over his face and sat up cautiously.

"Be quiet," Charles warned him. "The rangers are here."

"What are they doing?" Mitch peered over the top of the log.

"Shoveling dirt."

"On the fire?"

"Nah. Just on the stumps and little trees all around. It's hardly burning anymore, anyway."

"What are they doing that for?"

"Keeping it cool. So that any sparks that fly and happen to land won't burn into the timber, you know what I mean?"

"That's interesting."

Charles snorted. "It's their job, what's interesting about it?"

"Well, I thought you used water to put out a fire. I never thought you could use just a shovel."

"They also use a thing with an ax head on one end and a hoe on the other."

Mitch held his breath. Someone was passing

close-by. They heard branches swishing back and twigs snapping.

"Okay!" Mitch heard one man shout to the other. "We can go now. Nothing much left of it. Sure must have been pretty when it flared."

"Pretty! No fire is pretty to me. Not when you've been at it as long as I have."

"Mike!" another voice called.

"Yeah?"

"Looks like somebody's been hanging around the cabins here."

Mitch held himself still.

"Kids?"

"Hard to tell. Maybe."

"Well, they're gone now."

"Good riddance!"

"Yeah."

Mitch wriggled uncomfortably. Charles poked him.

"Good thing we got it fast."

"Couple of men coming down from Dutch Miller Gap saw the blaze and reported it. Some people staying down at Camp Brown called in about it, too. Rain's driving them all home."

"Bring the fire tools and let's get going. We don't have anything to worry about anymore. It's good as out."

"Too bad about the old hotel."

"Yeah. She was an old-timer."

Mitch pressed himself against the wet log. The voices moved past the log and were swallowed up in the wet foliage.

"They're gone," said Charles. He sat up, his hair plastered flat against his head by the rain, his shoulders hunched to keep the drops off his neck.

Mitch wiped the water dripping off his nose. "Where's the old guy?"

"Who cares?" said Charles. "Let's go up to the Coppermouth and warm up."

"Maybe that's where he went."

They dragged their stuff back to the cabin and dumped everything inside.

"Anyway they didn't find him either," said Mitch, and he quickly followed Charles up the trail past the steaming hole of the burned-down hotel.

chapter 18

THE MORNING PAPER plopped against the front door. Frank opened the door to pick it up. The night rain had wet everything down. He closed the door and glanced at the headlines.

Bernie was up and cheerful. His cheerfulness was an irritation. It wasn't fair to blame Bernie, Frank told himself. It wasn't Bernie's fault that Mitch had run away. Whose fault was it, he wondered. He tried to face the question honestly. But it was too much for him. Too early in the morning. He was too tired. It was too big.

"I checked with the rangers," Bernie was saying importantly. "They have an office right outside North Bend. They hear about everything that goes on in that area."

"What did they hear?" Frank's voice had a sharp edge.

"Nothing about Mitch. Woods are full of campers this time of year, the fellow I talked to said. So many people have been going hiking that they've had to cut down a whole section of trees for a parking lot. He said there are more than a hundred

places to hike to around there. There's a book list-
ing them."

"One hundred!" Miriam knelt to wipe up some
milk Joe had spilled.

"But the rain cleared most of the hikers and
campers out, is what he said," Bernie announced
triumphantly.

Miriam stood up.

"He said it rained so hard, there was not much
fire danger. He sounded pretty happy about that.
He says people never stay in the woods when it's
wet."

Miriam was looking out the window. It had
begun to rain again. Frank glanced at the clock on
the wall — and frowned when he saw it wasn't
there. Mitch would be home by noon, he told
himself, and he held on to the thought with all
corners of his mind.

"He could be home by noon." Miriam's voice
was lighter.

Bernie ruffled through the morning paper.
"Hey! Listen to this."

Frank looked over his shoulder. On the second
page of the newspaper was a photograph, a blown-
up snapshot of a youth standing at the top of a rock
canyon.

Bernie read aloud: "Poised high atop a granite
slide over which water tumbles into Lake Lipsi, ap-
proximately 20 miles north of North Bend, was a

19-year-old Yakima resident. Only seconds later he fell 900 feet to his death early Saturday morning."

"North Bend?" Miriam whispered. She stood rigidly, listening, her arms crooked stiffly at her sides.

"Two hiking companions said that he attempted to climb down the steep rock facing at Otter Slide Falls and slipped," Bernie continued.

"It says the picture was taken by a hiker who was across a small lake when the boy fell."

Frank gazed at the slender figure standing on top of the falls. Miriam looked and turned her head quickly away.

"Army helicopter summoned to scene and rushed victim to Seattle hospital," Bernie read. "Dead on arrival."

Dead on arrival. Frank looked into his cup of coffee.

Bernie flipped the pages over to the comic section. "Well, it wasn't Mitch," he said cheerily.

Miriam began to cry.

Hastily Frank pushed back his chair. "Come on, Bob," he said. "Let's have another look around. Like Jeff said, it isn't likely he'd go hiking by himself anyway."

"My name is Bernie," said Bernie, and followed him out to the car.

"Do you want me to drive?" Helpfully, Bernie put his hand on the door handle on the driver's side.

"All right."

"Where to?" Bernie backed the car out of the driveway; the tires touched the curb as they turned the corner.

Frank fastened his seat belt. "Let's go through the University District first."

Bernie headed down University Way. Frank recalled that he and Bob used to stroll along here. The post office was the same, but the University Book Store now embraced the stores on either side. And there were lots of new places. A beauty parlor for men. Two Steps Up, Arabesque — hippie shops. The customers lounged on the sidewalks. Long hair, fringed vests, bare feet.

Bernie headed up toward the freeway. There had been no freeway when he and Bob were kids, thought Frank. No Space Needle then either. The Smith Tower with its forty-two floors had been the highest building in the city, and there had been no bridges spanning Lake Washington. He and Bob used to take the ferry at the foot of Madison Street.

Frank sat up. "Madison Park," he said. "And Madrona."

"How do I get there?"

Frank leaned forward to catch the next big green directional sign. "Take the next exit. We'll cut on up to Broadway and hit into Madison. We can

110

follow Madison Street right on down to the lake."

Bob and he used to take their sleeping bags and camp right on the boulevard at Madison Park, he recalled. Kids didn't do that anymore. Bernie followed the boulevard that led halfway around Lake Washington. Frank scanned the shoreline. Families with bags of bread feeding ducks. Sailboats and water-skiers. Once he and Bob had rigged together a sailboat. Bob had been a real sailor. Frank stared out onto the blue lake, remembering. Bob had loved baseball. They used to take the street car to Sick's Stadium for the baseball games, and roller-skate down to the movies on Saturday.

The sound of a low siren interrupted Frank's recollections. He sat up, feeling the jerk of the seat belt. His eye caught the speedometer. "Slow down!" he shouted.

Bernie reluctantly removed his foot from the gas pedal. "What's the matter?" he said.

But Frank didn't have to answer. The white police car had pulled alongside them and the officer motioned to them to pull over.

Frank reached over and cranked down the window. They had been going 40 miles an hour in a 20-mile zone.

"Let me see your driver's license, please." Frank unsnapped his safety belt and reached into his back pocket.

"Not yours. The driver's."

Bernie was looking straight ahead. "Show him your driver's license," Frank said.

Bernie's hands remained on the wheel. "I haven't got a driver's license."

"But I thought —"

"I'm old enough. But my mother —"

Frank took a long deep breath. "Okay, officer," he said. "I guess it was my fault. I'll have to take the responsibility."

The officer had already taken out his book. "Driving without a license is a misdemeanor," he said. "And so is aiding and abetting a law violator."

"Officer, I didn't aid and abet —"

"This your car?"

"Yes."

"You let the kid drive?"

"Well, yes —"

The policeman flipped over a sheet in his book. "I'm giving you each one."

Frank took the wheel and drove home slowly. It had begun to rain again. Water was leaking in at the edge of the window on his side.

"Hand me the rag that's in the glove compartment, will you, Bob?"

"My name is Bernie," Bernie said, and flipped open the glove-compartment door.

Frank swabbed at the leak. "I know your name is

Bernie," he said, trying not to lose his temper. "I know who I'm talking to."

"No, you don't," Bernie said. "You keep calling me Bob, I'm Bernie. Bob is dead."

The blunt words cut through the fog in Frank's head. His fingers gripped the steering wheel tightly. Somehow, in his mind, Bob had never been dead.

He had never wanted to believe his brother was dead, just as he had refused to believe that Mitch had run away. It was easy not to believe what you didn't want to believe. Too easy. He gave a short laugh that scratched at his throat.

"All right," he said feeling tired and not young anymore. "I'll try to remember."

It was almost noon. They drove homeward in silence.

chapter 19

THE TRAIL TO THE COPPERMOUTH was soft with rain. Mitch followed Charles up the steep path. Their feet slid on the damp roots, and churned up the loamier sections.

The waterfall roared below them. Raindrops flew from the leaves of the boughs which brushed the path, and showered their faces and necks. When the sun came out, vapor began to rise from the wet growth all around them.

The boys pulled off their clothes quickly in front of the warm mouth of the cave. An old jacket lay neatly folded on the ledge that formed the rock step up into the opening of the Coppermouth. Below it was a pair of trousers and muddy tennis shoes.

The boys peered into the dim opening. The steam warmed their faces as they leaned far in.

"Hey! You in there?" Mitch called. But he heard only the echo and then the trickle and the soft *plop, plop* of water.

"You, there!" shouted Charles into the long cavern. His voice returned eerily.

"Probably can't hear you," said Mitch. "Water

swallows sounds easy." He blinked into the steamy interior. The cave went in about twenty feet. They held on to each other as they stepped into the hot water. The water came to their mid-thighs at its deepest point. The cave bottom was uneven with shales of rock. Mitch stepped forward carefully. The ceiling rose to a peak above him.

When Mitch's eyes had become accustomed to the darkness in the cave, he looked for the spring opening. The water came out of a crack in the rock in the left wall almost two thirds of the way in. The copper vein had decorated the walls with smears of yellows and rusts and reds. Coppermouth. It was a good name.

Mitch saw the man first. He was lying on his back asleep. His head rested on a ledge and his feet floated in the shallow water.

They waded along, stretching their arms out to touch the cave walls as they took each step. They had to step over the sleeping form to reach the end, and step over him again to come back. He didn't even wake up.

"Let's sit out in the tub awhile," said Mitch. "He must have been up all night watching the hotel burn."

Charles climbed out of the cave opening, and Mitch behind him. Charles bent over the pile of clothes.

"Hey, what are you doing?" said Mitch.

Charles didn't answer. He went quickly through the pockets. He pulled out some coins, an empty tobacco pouch, bits and scraps of paper, a stick of chewing gum, and the metal pipe. With an expression of disgust he stuck everything back in again. "Not even a good joint," he said.

Charles stepped into the big tub. The water was running steadily into it through the old hose.

Mitch climbed in too and sat down in the hot water. The wooden cedar tub was a long one. The boys sat facing each other, their legs stretched out. Mitch closed his eyes.

"How long do you think that guy is going to sleep in there?" Charles said after a while.

"He's probably tired," Mitch said. "You'd be tired too if you had sat up all night."

"He probably came to take the cure. That's what people used to come up here for. The hot springs were supposed to cure everything. I heard somewhere that people came up here on crutches and with canes, and after they had bathed in the Coppermouth for a while, they walked out — cured."

"I don't notice any crutches or canes lying around."

"There was supposed to have been a stack of them on the top floor of the hotel. You can't prove it by me, though. I didn't go up to see."

"You think it really works?"

Charles regarded Mitch lazily. "Why not? Anybody who'd come way out to this place and build a hotel must have figured he had something going for him."

"It couldn't have worked," Mitch pointed out. "Or else the hotel still would have been running."

"It was running, more or less."

"Where are the customers?"

"Him," Charles said. "In there. He's a customer."

"Some customer," said Mitch.

"I'm cooked," said Charles.

They climbed out of the tub hurriedly and ran down to the cold pool of the stream. They splashed around in its icy waters and when their legs began to feel numb, they ran back again quickly and immersed themselves in the tub.

"I like it here," said Mitch.

"All the comforts of home." Charles took a mouthful of the water and spewed it into the air. "Ptooey! Tastes like bath water."

"That's what it is," said Mitch.

"No, it's spring water. Just like the stream. Good to drink, if you like water hot."

"Only when it's tea," said Mitch. The thought of his mother and father sitting at the kitchen table drinking tea came to his mind. "Personally I don't like tea," he said loudly.

"Me neither," said Charles.

Their heads both turned toward the cave opening, although no sound had emerged. The light steam vapor gently blew out of the triangular opening in the solid face of the rock wall. Above the pointed mouth, great jags of layered rock formed a foothold for ferns, liverworts, and lichens. Moss grew there several inches thick.

Charles stood up, flung his leg over the side of the big tub, and leaned into the cavern opening. "Hey in there! You going to stay all day!"

"Aw, leave him alone," said Mitch.

Charles settled down into the wooden tub again. "Do you think he's going to sleep all day?"

"Well, he paid you, didn't he?"

Charles grimaced. "He spent all day yesterday picking wild huckleberries. Only he said they weren't as good as wortleberries."

"I never heard of anything called wortleberries."

"Did you ever hear of salmonberries?"

"Sure. They're orange colored. Taste blah."

"Bet you never ate salal berries."

"Not when I could find wild huckleberries." Mitch rested the back of his neck on the edge of the tub and looked up at the sky. It was turning blue again. A wet blue. He could see mountain peaks.

"One day soon I'm going to hike up that ridge and go right to Canada," said Charles dreamily.

"Or maybe Mexico," Mitch said, feeling drowsy

and comfortable. "Personally I don't think I'd much like to hike all the way to Mexico."

"Why not?"

"I like it here."

Charles pulled himself up, spilling glops of water onto the rocks under the tub. Mitch opened his eyes.

"Do you always talk in circles?"

Mitch sat up too, his skin feeling uncomfortably warm. "I don't think so."

"Yes, you do. You talk in circles." Charles scratched his head. "That's sort of interesting, you know what I mean?"

"Thank you."

"I mean it's a dumb way to talk."

"So is saying the same thing over and over again."

"You don't have to listen. You can go to sleep like the guy in the cave."

They both turned their heads.

The man must have moved up from the back of the cave. He was lying closer to the mouth, floating. They could see his feet bobbing gently toward the entrance.

"Skinny feet," said Mitch.

Charles snickered. He stood up suddenly, climbed out of the tub, and crept to the cave mouth. Unexpectedly, he rose, whooping and hollering, and pulled the man out by his feet. The sound of

Charles's shouts rolled over the promontory and fell away into the deep river.

But the man just lay sprawled where he landed. For a moment they stared at the white skinny body. It did not move.

Mitch felt the hairs on the back of his head begin to bristle. "What's the matter with him?"

"Holy cow!" breathed Charles. "He's dead."

chapter 20

WHEN FRANK CAME into the kitchen, his wife was standing on an old chair. She was putting some cracked plates on the cupboard shelves.

"What are you doing?" he said in surprise.

"Unpacking," she said without stopping her work.

He saw the carton on the counter then. It was the one he had marked carefully for the Salvation Army pickup truck. *Kitchen Giveaway,* it said. *This Side Up.* She was putting everything back on the shelves.

He listened to the click of plate on plate, staring at the odd stack of mismatched cups and saucers. The kitchen chair scraped as she pulled it to the next shelf.

He looked at her dumbly.

"Tell me everything will be just fine," she said bitterly.

He said with a desperate feeling, "Wait. It's going to work out. Everything will be just fine."

She turned around to laugh at him. A scornful sound. Then she went right on with her unpacking.

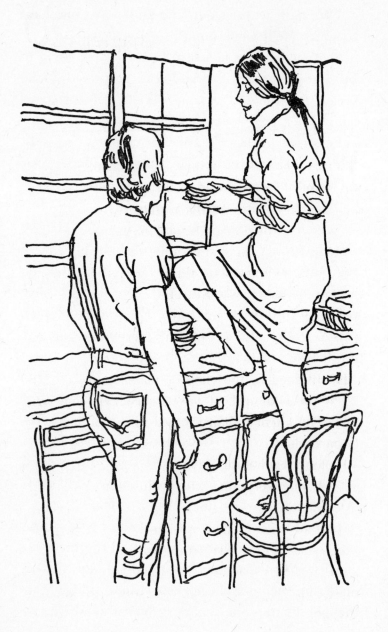

"We have to sit it out," he said. "We just have to wait. He'll come home."

She nodded. "And when he does we're going to be here as usual. Everything is going to be the same — or almost the same. We'll go someday — later. We can go next year. There's plenty of time."

He shook his head. "For twenty years, I've been telling myself that there is plenty of time. That we'll go someday. Every year, we say 'next year.' "

"It isn't as if we have to go," she said.

"I've quit my job," he reminded her. "They've already got my replacement. We've already rented the house and signed a lease. Our stuff is on the way. Our plane tickets are paid for. Our bills are paid. Our car is sold — or will be when they pick it up. They've been holding the job for me in Tel Aviv. They're depending on me."

She shouted, "What about Mitch?!"

He didn't shout back. His voice came out thin and raspy. He felt as if he had no voice at all. He tried to make his feelings understandable to her. "Maybe we should have listened more. But we did what we thought was right. For him as well as us. We can't change our minds now."

Her answer was to take another item out of the box and place it defiantly back upon the shelf.

Miriam had made up her mind. When Miriam made up her mind, no one could budge her, thought Frank. She was as stubborn as Mitch.

chapter 21

Mitch felt the steam rising from the tub, warm against his face. He heard the noise of the foaming white water pounding down in the gorge behind. He saw the shimmering greens of the hanging mosses and ferns over the opening of the Coppermouth.

Life was movement, thought Mitch. Life was noise. Life was greens and yellows and blues and reds. Life was standing up and fighting back. He remembered how awfully still the man had lain in there. Dead. He shivered.

He guessed he had known all along that he was dead, thought Mitch. He just hadn't wanted to know it.

Hurriedly Mitch rose. He climbed out of the big tub and began pulling on his clothes. He didn't let himself look at the naked dead man.

"How long do you think he's been like that?"

"Who cares?" Charles was using his teeth to unknot the twists in his shoelaces. "We've got to get out of here, you know what I mean?"

"We can't just leave him here," said Mitch doubtfully.

"Why not?"

"You can't just leave someone dead."

"He's nothing to us."

"He's human."

"Was, you mean, was. He's dead now."

"That's what I meant," said Mitch. "That's why. He was a human being. We can't just walk off and leave him."

"We don't even know his name," said Charles. "We don't know where he came from or where he was going to. All we did was find him." Charles waved his arms around in a vague sort of way. "He's not our responsibility, you know what I mean?"

Responsibility. Mitch had never thought about its meaning. He looked at the dead man.

"Everyone has responsibility for everyone else," Mitch heard himself saying. "That's what being human means."

He walked over the stones in his bare feet and yanked at the rolled blanket lying under the dead man's clothes. He flapped it out and carefully spread the tattered gray covering over the naked figure.

Charles pulled his shirt over his head. "Hurry up!"

Mitch walked back, stuck his feet into his shoes, and tied the laces firmly.

"What we've got to do is go out to North Bend and go to the police station —"

"You're crazy!" yelled Charles. "I'm not going

anywhere near any police station. My father would just love to have me walk into a police station!"

Mitch hesitated.

"Neither of us is that dumb, you know what I mean?" Charles said quickly.

Mitch listened to the water falling down into the gorge. "Some things are more important than other things," he said.

"Nothing is more important to me than me." Charles stood up. He moved swiftly across the promontory and headed down the trail.

"We've got to," Mitch said. He plunged after Charles. Their feet slipped and slid on the muddy trail. As Charles leaped on ahead of him, the branches slapped back at Mitch's head. Charles laughed. Mitch stumbled on the slippery roots but kept close behind him.

They ran past the black patch of the burned-down hotel and reached the cabins together. Charles began to drag his stuff out. He rolled everything into his sleeping bag. Mitch put his pack together and hoisted it onto his back.

"We've got to do what we can do," Mitch said.

Charles slung his stuff across his shoulders and whirled away down the trail.

"We have to." Mitch followed Charles.

They moved along, one behind the other, swiftly. The spongy path absorbed the sound of their steps and the wet green foliage, full of pearls in the sunlight, sprayed their necks as they brushed by.

Charles didn't stop until he came to the bisecting trail marker. Ahead was the fir-needle path that led down to the log bridge, past the empty miners' shacks, up the rutted red-earth road to the spur where Charles had parked his father's car. Behind them was the way to the Coppermouth.

CASCADE CREST TRAIL the marker said. Charles stopped to stare at it.

The letters were hand-cut, deeply etched into the thick cedar slab. Mitch could see the flat cuts of the knife that had been used to chisel out the letters. The hollow spaces had been brushed with an orange stain.

The silence of the forest surrounded them. A bird, close-by but out of sight, whistled; a squirrel darted up a tree trunk. Great Douglas firs grew high into the sky around them. Suddenly the roaring waterfall, the burned-down hotel, and the Coppermouth seemed a million miles away. Mitch took a deep breath.

"We could take the Cascade Crest Trail, you know," Charles said softly. "If we stick together we could go all the way up to Canada." His eyes gleamed at Mitch in the sunlight. "Or maybe even down to Mexico — you know what I mean?"

chapter 22

I'M GOING TO TAKE BERNIE home with me," Bernie's mother said.

She was a large, broad-shouldered woman with a strong voice and naturally red cheeks. To look at her, thought Frank, you wouldn't know that inside that big frame beat a fearful heart.

"He might as well come home with me," she said.

Frank glanced at his wife. She had not talked to him directly since morning. She would speak to him only when she had to and then her glance would go over his shoulder, fasten on his ear, or skim the top of his head. She did not meet his glance now. He sighed. The plane would be leaving without them tomorrow morning.

"Does he want to?" he challenged his sister-in-law with care.

Louise laughed at the question. "Why shouldn't he want to?"

Frank wondered whether he should try to answer that. He felt he owed Bernie something. He didn't quite know what, but something.

"Why don't you let Bernie go ahead by himself? He could stay on a kibbutz. That's what he planned to do anyway."

Louise gave him a pinched smile. "Your son doesn't want to go — what makes you think mine does?"

"He says he does," Frank pointed out.

She laughed knowingly. "That's only because he knows I don't want him to."

Frank looked thoughtfully at his sister-in-law.

She had bombarded her son all his life with cautions and warnings: Be careful, don't run too fast, you'll fall down! Don't climb so high, you might break a leg! Keep away from the window, you'll catch cold! Watch out, you'll hurt yourself!

"The more I worry, the more pleased Bernie is," Louise said. "Sometimes I think he tries to frighten me on purpose."

"Why do you think that?" Miriam asked.

Louise flushed. "Two years ago Bernie threatened to quit school as soon as he could so he could train to be a fireman. Last year he decided he would go on to college in case he wanted to be an airline pilot. And only three months ago, do you know what he wrote the government for training information about? Being an astronaut! Now he says he wants to be an astronaut!" She shuddered.

Frank couldn't help it; he laughed.

"It's nothing to laugh about," Louise said angrily. Her eyes filled with tears. "Does he have to be like that?"

Frank felt sorry for his sister-in-law.

"Perhaps he has to," Frank said slowly. "Perhaps he has to be like that to prove he's not afraid. Maybe that's the only way he can run away from you."

Louise gasped. Miriam raised her head.

"Maybe we don't look at things the way our children do," he said. "Maybe we should."

Thoughtfully, he walked around the dining room table. He looked at the scarred top. He gazed upon it and did not feel any rush of anger. The dining room table seemed suddenly irrelevant. He kept looking at it.

Frank saw the newsprint indelibly laminated to the table top. He saw Mitch laying the newspaper sheets down one by one, thoroughly covering every inch. Mitch never hurried about doing anything. He never saw any reason for hurrying.

"What's the matter?" said Miriam, finally looking at him directly.

"Nothing." Frank moved quickly down the stairs. He pushed open the door to Mitch's room and stood there looking in. He didn't know what he was looking for or what he expected to find.

The room was empty. The piles of stuff Mitch had left all over the floor were packed and had gone. He remembered now that socks and underclothes had made up one pile. Winter woolens were in another. Shirts and pullovers had been shoved under the chair. All the shoes had been in a jumble by the door. He had only seen that everything was all over the floor.

They had never looked at things the same way, thought Frank. He went back upstairs, thinking about it.

"They must have had holes in them," he said standing in the middle of the kitchen.

His wife gave him a strange look.

"The socks Mitch threw in the wastebasket. Did they have holes?"

"Oh those." She sounded guilty. "They weren't a pair, I discovered. I must have given the mates away by mistake."

Louise was paying no attention. She sat, her hands folded, staring out the window. Miriam started to hang Mitch's picture of airplanes back up on the wall. He stood there looking at it.

"They forgot to pack it in," she said, and pounded at the nail determinedly.

Louise turned around. She regarded the picture without any particular interest. "They look like ducks."

"Not ducks," said Frank. "Airplanes."

Louise looked at it again and shrugged. "I guess it's all in the way you look at it."

Frank took another look at the picture. He

stepped back, half closed his eyes, and squinted at it.

Suddenly he saw ducks winging across the blue sky. He opened his eyes wide and stared.

"Those *are* ducks!" he said in surprise. "Not airplanes — ducks!"

Unexpectedly, Miriam laughed.

chapter 23

MITCH LEANED his bicycle against the garage door, stepped carefully around his father's car sitting in the driveway and walked slowly up the back porch steps to the kitchen door.

Through the window, he saw that everybody was in the kitchen. He saw the back of his Aunt Louise's head. Her hair was as fluttery as the handkerchief in her hands. Bernie hunched near her uneasily, a grown dog on a too-tight leash. The smug, know everything look seemed to have gone from his face. Unexpectedly Mitch felt a little sorry for his cousin Bernie.

Mitch saw his mother at the stove lifting off the teakettle. He looked at his father sitting at the corner of the kitchen table waiting for his tea.

Mitch stood there, hesitating.

Charles had driven his car glumly over the narrow mountain road back to the main highway.

"All we have to do is tell them where to find him," said Mitch as they rode into the town. North Bend was as flat as the bottom of a soup plate.

Mount Si rose startlingly close, a black hulk resting on the outskirts.

They waited for the light to change and crawled through the town's main street. The Mount Si Cleaners had a Swiss-style front. The tavern and the bakery had a similar look with bright colors, flower boxes, and balconies. A place to eat was called The Little Chalet. There were eleven service stations, five restaurants, a bank — and a police station.

"Over there," Mitch directed.

Charles swerved to the curb and came to a quick stop.

"You know what, Berson?"

"What?"

"You stink."

"I thought you had no sense of smell."

"Well, I must have been wrong."

Mitch got out of the car. "All we have to do —"

The car jerked forward, screeched around the corner, and was gone. A knob as big as a fist suddenly filled Mitch's throat. He walked resolutely toward the police station.

They didn't even ask him his name. They told him to sit down and they called the Radio Dispatching Room for the sheriff. The sheriff must have been nearby; he came in a newly washed white Plymouth with a sheriff's emblem on its door. The car's inside was blue and there was a red dome light on top. The sheriff stopped to wipe a speck off his windshield before getting out of the car.

Inside the police station, he listened to what Mitch had to say and looked at him consideringly.

"You say he's dead, huh?"

Mitch nodded.

The sheriff ambled over to the desk and picked up the telephone.

Mitch felt the sweat under his armpits and on the middle of his back.

"Pete?" the sheriff said into the telephone. "There's a kid here who says there's a dead man up at Coppermouth."

The man on the other end of the line must have asked a question. The sheriff turned his head, regarded Mitch a moment, and murmured back into the telephone. He listened a moment longer. "Pick you up. Ten minutes."

Mitch felt the air coming back easily into his lungs. He started to back out.

"Hey you!"

Mitch stopped.

"We'll want you to go back with us," the sheriff said. "Show us the place."

Helplessly, Mitch nodded. He had to go back the whole twenty-six miles with them. He led them over the log bridge through the grown-over trail, past the two shacks and the burned-down hotel, and up the steep climb to the Coppermouth.

"Dead, all right," said Pete.

The sheriff began to go methodically through the pile of clothes. He turned the pockets inside out and sniffed at them.

Mitch walked to the edge of the promontory. He looked across at the jungle green wall, felt the spray of the water gushing over the slippery rocks, and read the paper sign stuck on a stick at his feet. The rain had streaked it but you could still read it all right. *Beware.*

"Let's go," ordered the sheriff. "We'll send the coroner back for the body."

Mitch bent down and twisted the stick more securely into the dirt. Then he led the men back down the trail.

They stopped to look at the place where the hotel had stood. The sheriff and Pete poked around the ashes. They looked inside the two cabins and kicked at the pile of empty tin cans. The sheriff wrote some things down in his notebook.

"What were you doing around here?" the sheriff asked suddenly.

Mitch swallowed. "Hiking."

That's all they asked him.

Nobody said anything much on the way back. The sheriff said he was going to have to wash his car all over again. They drove Mitch back to the gas station where he had left his bicycle.

"Say," said Mitch as he got out of the car. "What day is this?"

The sheriff looked at him curiously. "Monday. It's been Monday all day."

"And tomorrow is Tuesday," Pete said.

Tuesday. Mitch looked at his bike a moment without seeing it.

"Thanks," he said then, and unlocked it. The sheriff's car still stood there. Mitch glanced at it uneasily.

The sheriff stuck his head out the window. "Hop in," he said, "we'll run you home."

Mitch hadn't planned on going home. Not until after Tuesday.

"One good turn deserves another," the sheriff said. "We'll put your bike in the trunk."

Mitch stood with his hands hanging down at his sides while Pete and the sheriff fitted his bike into the large trunk.

"Thanks," he said drily.

Then they drove him into Seattle and dropped him off in front of his house.

Mitch looked through the kitchen window.

He noticed his picture hanging on a new place on the wall. Through the doorway into the next room he could see the dining room table. He stared at it. The top had been sanded down. It was bare wood. Clean. The glued newspaper was all gone. It must have taken a lot of work to sand the top down, Mitch reflected. He could already hear his father yelling at him.

Automatically, Mitch braced himself for the expected outburst. Then somehow he knew his father wasn't going to yell. Not about the table. Not anymore. That was over and done with.

But there would always be something to yell about, Mitch reminded himself. He and his father would never see anything exactly the same way, not at the first look anyway. Sooner or later his father would be yelling at him about something again. That wouldn't ever change.

He looked at his father sitting there. He had never before noticed how much like him Bernie looked. They could have been father and son, Mitch thought, and wished he hadn't noticed.

Mitch stood there for another moment looking in.

The curlers were gone from his mother's hair. So were the poofs and waves. Her hair hung lank and straight down over her ears. She didn't seem to care. Mitch watched her pour the hot tea into a cup, set it on an unmatched saucer, and hand it to his father. He saw his father blow at it a little and then not bother to drink it.

His mother and father wouldn't have gone without him, Mitch thought. No matter how much they wanted to go, they wouldn't have left without him. He felt his surprise at knowing that, and then it did not surprise him at all.

With an odd feeling of relief, Mitch opened the door.